ANCIENT DREAMS, NEWBORN VISIONS

BY

JOSEPH A. WAILES

OUTLAW PRESS
RAWHIDE, TEXAS

ISBN 978-0-9916454-3-5
PRINTED AND BOUND IN
THE UNITED STATES OF AMERICA

OUTLAW PRESS
2980 PHYLLIS LANE
RAWHIDE, TEXAS
75234-6425

THE WINNER OF THE HUMAN RACE

BY

JOSEPH A. WAILES

I_WHEN LIGHT BECAME A MAN

II_THE LONGEST NIGHT

III_ANCIENT DREAMS, NEWBORN VISIONS

IV_WAR OF THE BOOK

V_THE THIRD UNIVERSAL EVENT HORIZON

VI_HARVEST MOON

VII_TOO GOOD TO BE UNTRUE

BOOKS AVAILABLE AT OUTLAW PRESS

TABLE OF CONTENTS

FOREWORD – STRANGE HORIZONS

When this expedition into uncharted regions of hidden wisdom and mysteries yet unexplored began, I had no clear idea where it would lead. I was shown things I could never have imagined, and granted perceptions and perspectives I had never before experienced. I still do not understand a lot of it, even now. I only wrote what I was shown to write.

I realize that many of the concepts included are unusual, and may seem impossible. Of course, I ask you to remember that Jesus Christ told us that with God, nothing shall be called impossible. Ask Him to guide your own explorations, and, as always, check these ideas out, as in agreement with the Word of God. Perhaps it will be that our good Lord will show you some of the same things He showed me, or perhaps He has a whole different set of dreams and visions for you. You follow Him, wherever He leads you, and you will not get lost.

THE FIRST DREAM THAT I CAN REMEMBER

The dream that I recall as my very earliest intense dream was given when I was either four or five years old, since I remember that we were living in the house we had in Houston. I remember waking up frightened, and going into the den where my Dad and Mom were watching television. It was most likely about eight or so in the evening, since the year was 1955 or 1956, and little boys that young went to bed early, and television programs did not broadcast after 10:00 P.M.

I only recall a little bit of it now, over 50 years later, but I do remember that I was outside in a very big, open field. The grass was not extremely tall, but only about a foot or so. The vegetation was mostly brown and yellow, as in the color of wintertime fields. The field went as far

8

as I could see, in every direction, and there were no buildings, trees, or even hills or rises of the terrain. It was all flat and level.

I knew I was all alone, and that scared me. Remember, I was only four or five at the time. I tried to guess which way was home, and started walking in that direction.

Suddenly, I noticed a movement in the grass, off to one side. I froze. As I stared in the direction of the flicker of motion, I saw the side of a brown, patterned snake slide through the gap in the weeds!

I immediately turned to run away, but only had stumbled a few panic-driven steps through the brush, when I saw a large coiled snake just in front of me. I did not notice what kind of snake it was; I just turned to run still another direction.

The pattern repeated itself over and over, no matter which way I turned. There was no escape, and no rescue, either. I was defenseless, and knew that eventually, they would get me.

Then the sweet mercy was given to me by the good Lord, and I was allowed to wake up, and walk into the other room, where my magnificent Dad and Mom were there to comfort me, and calm me down. If I recall correctly, my Mom said that it was because she had let me have two chocolate chip cookies after supper, instead of the usual one. I doubt her theory, and I doubted it the minute she said it, all those years ago, but a frightened little boy did not want to make a debate with the people to whom he came for comfort and help.

Many times in the course of my life since then, I have had vivid dreams that indeed did come to pass, often times, with stunning accuracy, though there may have been years between the dream and the manifestation. That particular dream has never happened yet, at least, not literally, though some situations and environments have felt much the same. I still have the hope that even if that dream ever does materialize, perhaps this time I might wake up in Heaven. It will be wonderful to see Dad and Mom again.

TRAUMA TRAIN

The precise age when this dream occurred is uncertain, but it can be narrowed down to somewhere between seven and ten years of age. It is not linked by association to any other major events in my life at the time, so I cannot accurately pinpoint the year.

I remember waking up, with tears on my pillow, one scary night after a dream where I had suddenly found myself in a jumbled horror of a huge train wreck, with those long, shiny train cars all scattered not far away from the track, some on one side of it, some on the other. They were even stacked on top of each other, in a few cases, and the line of derailed, gleaming passenger cars disappeared in the distance, both ahead, and behind, as far as I could see. I do not know how the wreck happened. I have no memory of that, but I remember it was extremely realistic, with thick, richly scented pine trees all along the tracks, and very bright sunlight, and a cool, fresh breeze, with a few big white puffy clouds in a blue sky. I remember it was ghostly quiet, except for the whisper of the breeze, and the sound of my own footsteps crunching alongside the track in the gravel there.

That was not the scary part. Everywhere I looked, there were dead folks. There were hundreds of them, as far as I could see, down the track. The odd thing was that none of them were still alive. Every single person was sprawled here or there, randomly placed from the impact, and not a single one of them breathed any more. There was also a very great amount of blood all over almost the whole scene. Only the gleaming, silver train cars seemed to be completely clean.

I also remember that I could not find my parents. Somehow that seemed very important to me. I guess, since I was only ten years old, or younger, in my waking life, the same type of priorities still held during my dream. I know when anything distressful or threatening happened in real life, I always went to them for help. They always helped the very best they could, too.

I remember that when I waked, I went quietly out of my bed, still dripping tears, down the hall, and looked into my parents' room. It was sometime in the deep hours of the night, and they were both sound asleep. I blinked away at the tears, holding my breath to be quiet, and trying to see if they were breathing. About the time I had to take a breath myself, my Dad suddenly snorted a snort, and rolled over, without really waking up at all. I was never so glad to hear anyone snore as much as at that time.

I wiped my eyes, and went back to my bed. In those years my eyes could see very well in the dark, and I did not need flashlights to find my way around with the lights off.

I did not really want to go back to bed, and back to sleep, and maybe have the same painful dream again, but I was only about ten years old, and did not have any concept of going into the kitchen to make a cup of coffee, and then think it over a while. I did not know what else to do, so I got back in bed, and said some sort of prayer, and fell back asleep. The next morning, I did remember the dream, but never told anyone at all about it, until now, as I write this story.

I still never understood the message of that dream, yet, but so far, at least, it has never come true. I do not know if it will in the future. The only part that did manifest over the years is that I did indeed remain in the Earth many years after the graduation (to Heaven) of my parents. I know they both ran their full courses, though, and I am extremely proud of each of them. I do not wake up with tears on my pillow anymore. I miss them, but I still have my own course to finish. I expect to see them again, after that.

CARNIVAL OF CRUELTY

This dream happened sometime after the age of fifty. I did not write any of it down until now. It was extremely strange, and frightening, but the Lord keeps putting it in my heart to write it, in case someone else is experiencing anything similar.

I was in some sort of a small tent, like a little circus tent, maybe 15 feet in diameter. I was standing in the very center of the tent, which had a concrete floor. There was no furniture, or any other object of decoration, or function. The only thing in the tent, besides me, was the iron rings anchored to the concrete floor, and the strong chains which were locked to them. The other ends of the chains were shackles, and manacles, and a solid iron neck collar. They were all fastened tightly around my wrists, ankles, and throat. There was a single harsh light bulb hanging a few feet above my head. I was naked, and very cold, and scared.

There was one other object attached to me, also. Locked around my private parts was a sort of metal box, with some blinking red lights, and also a hand grenade made into the box, but partly visible in the dim light. I did not dare to touch the terrible thing, since I did not know what it would take to detonate the grenade, and I certainly did not want to find out. I tried to suppress my terror, since the extreme cold already was making me shiver some, anyway, and I knew if I lost my tight grip on my tiny little last shred of calmness, I would start shaking violently all over. I could not risk that.

Somehow I knew I had been held prisoner there for a very long time, maybe even several years. It seemed like I had just waked up, and found myself standing there. I did not consciously recall any experience of having been tortured, but something in the very inmost center of me knew that was what had indeed happened, not once, but thousands of times, over and over. Part of me also knew it would never stop, unless someone came to get me out. I knew I could never escape on my own, or else I already would have done so.

I truly did not want to be a cry-baby about it all, but I was broken, and realized the rest of my years would only be more of the same, or even worse.

I do not recall if I cried, or not, or if I prayed, or not, but suddenly, with absolutely no warning, the flap of the tent was pulled open, and in flooded a squad of four men. Three took up positions at even spacing around the sides of the tent, facing the door, and the fourth held the flap open with one hand, while his other held a nasty looking machine gun pointed outside. The soldier nodded his head as another person also came inside. All of the soldiers had been dressed in brown and green camouflage, with full arms and equipment, including helmets. The last arrival was a Man in maybe His mid thirties, extremely strong, and perfectly fit, with a full dark beard, and thick dark hair longer than military, about shoulder length. He wore a green and brown flannel shirt, and blue jeans with cargo pockets, and also had on combat boots. He was not wearing a gun, but had a huge Bowie knife strapped to His leg. He looked at me, and smiled, and said, "Don't worry. We're here to help!"

At that point, I know hot tears rushed down my cheeks, and I think I tried to say "Thank You!" I do not remember all the details.

One of the soldiers handed Him a cloak, which He quickly draped around my shoulders, and the instant and complete warmth allowed me to stop shivering and trembling, and I took a deep breath, and began to relax a little.

He put a hand upon my shoulder, looked me deep in the eye, and said, "Now stay calm. I want you to take a deep breath, when I say now, and close your eyes, and try not to move at all." I nodded.

He said the word "Release!" and the chains fell free, and hit the concrete with loud clangs. I tried to stand still.

He looked me in the eye, and said, "Ready? Okay, now!"

I took a quick, deep breath, slammed my eyes shut tight, and froze in place, trying to become motionless. There was a muffled explosion, and a very bright flash, which I still saw through my closed eyelids, and I had the brief image of the Man holding in His right hand a flaming, writhing, hissing ball of snakes, all of which kept trying to bite Him. Their efforts were in vain, though, since every time one tried, it broke its' fangs, but could not penetrate His skin. In only a split second, He hurled the whole huge writhing ball of deadly snakes down into and through the floor, while the sound of their screaming curses faded as though they were falling down into a deep well. Through all of this, which was over in about three seconds, the soldiers did not move at all, and neither did I.

As soon as the snakes were gone, one of the soldiers came over to me and dressed me in a camouflage combat outfit, just like theirs, except they did not give me a gun. Instead, the Man handed me a Bowie knife just like His, only a little bit smaller. I strapped it on my thigh, too, just like Him. As I stood up, completely dressed, and now, armed, too, I looked Him in the eye, and said calmly, "Thank You, Lord!"

He smiled, and said, "Move quickly, now. We have other places where We want you to fight."

I nodded, and we all moved quickly out of the door, and began working our way out of the circus grounds, moving unseen from cover to cover. I recall wondering why He did not want to reveal His presence, since He could single handedly whip the entire army of hell, and had already done it many times before. I do not know His reasoning, but I did follow His orders, and moved as quietly and quickly as the squad of angels with me. I do not know at just what point He left, but while we were still rescuing me, He vanished from us, but the four combat angels stayed with me all the way out. We had to run, we had to jump, we had to climb, we had to balance precariously across log bridges, but, at last we were clear. The circus area itself was very large, and I somehow knew many millions of other people were still trapped there. Most of them were so out of it that they did not even know that they were being held prisoner. Some of them liked it, and delighted in the ugliness of it all. I never have been sure why He came to save me.

As we were leaving, the sky began to grow lighter and clearer, and continued to improve, the farther away we went. All along the escape route, we encountered no resistance at all, which might have seemed unusual, until I remembered that He was supervising this mission. Maybe that's what He vanished to attend to, ensuring that the enemy soldiers would be busy with other things.

Finally we were all clear, and I found myself standing there in a small group with the soldiers, and they were all suddenly dressed in uniforms that resembled Navy khaki officers' outfits. They all had some sort of gold stars on their collar lapels. My jaw dropped. The equivalent rank of Admirals? In the Army of Heaven?!

Then I smiled as I heard Him chuckle in my mind, and He said, "Why should My Admirals being assigned to do this surprise you? There was a long list of volunteers, but these had the most seniority. Besides all of that, the Commander-in-Chief of the Army of Heaven was there in Person, too, wasn't I?"

The mighty angels were also smiling. They had also heard His Words. I thanked them for their help, and asked, "Now what?"

Again, His Words rang in my mind. He said, "I will give you orders from now on, minute by minute, by My Word, and by My Holy Spirit. The angels will still take their commands straight from Me, but they are assigned to you, from this day forward, until I return. Though you may not perceive their presence, they will always be near you, though I will always be closer still."

THE BIG WOODEN HOUSE

This dream happened sometime in my early fifties. I cannot pinpoint the year more accurately than that, since I do not remember any real world events that corresponded to this dream, at the time.

I watched as the same lot, upon which I had been allowed to grow up, since five years old, began to have a brand new four story gigantic wooden house crafted upon the old lot. I remember the inside of it was a wonderful maze of interconnecting rooms and hallways. There were some large rooms, and some small. There were spiral staircases, straight staircases, a couple of fireman-type poles, skylights, huge view windows, outside decks and porches, an observatory in the very top, with a new large home-size telescope, an indoor pool at the ground floor, and a three car garage incorporated into the main structure of the house. There was a fireplace on every floor, and also a central vaulted opening that went at two places from the first floor all the way to the skylights at the roof level.

The entire massive building was somehow fit precisely into this same little suburban lot. I have no idea how much it cost to buy the code variances it would have required. The total cost of the project was way past my ability to understand.

The whole structure was crafted of many types of wood, from the ordinary, to the exotic. It was all finished, skilled carpentry, done by some of the finest in the trade. None of the wood was painted, though much of it was stained with mild tone changes for special emphasis on the wood grain patterns, and all of it was clear-coated with a type of almost indestructible high-tech coating, which protected the wood, and also fire-proofed the entire thing.

The ground floor also had a lot of indoor illumination, with enormous clear polymer windows, storm-proof, and bullet-proof. There was additional light from daylight colored lights, and the large skylights. This allowed a special type of St. Augustine grass to thrive there, and made a giant indoor backyard for the dog and the cat a reality. A lot of fresh air was constantly flowing through the whole ground floor, warmed in winter, cooled in summer. The artificial lights timed with the outdoor sun by a simple photocell, wired backwards. Sun down meant lights out.

I remember that it was a lot of interesting fun to wander around in it, and I kept finding work crews of two or three folks wiring things, plumbing things, connecting things, installing things, and finishing things. For the most part they ignored me, unless they needed to pass through a narrow spot with something or other, in which cases they always politely and carefully worked their way past, or around me, not scratching any of the wood, or even bumping into me. I remember going into the kitchen, making a turkey sandwich and a cup of fresh coffee, and wandering around looking at all the things being installed and finished up everywhere, and it occurred to me that there must be at least two or three dozen people working inside the house! There was a bit of construction noise, but it was not anything like one would expect. Nevertheless, the work seemed to be progressing very smoothly and quickly. I do not know how I knew it was supposed to be my house, except that it was situated upon my little lot, and all the craftsmen treated me with a lot of respect, like they knew I was the homeowner, but they also knew I would keep my mouth shut, and stay out of their way, and get them whatever tools or equipment they needed. They knew if I wanted something changed or done differently, I would just politely ask them to accomplish it, and they would very agreeably do it right away. It was cool, but a house like that will almost certainly never belong to me in this present world. I would maybe say it was beyond my wildest dream-house, but I guess it actually was my wildest dream-house, at least so far. I think next time I will try more for the western slopes of the Colorado Rockies, or the Norwegian Fiords, or Hawaii. Maybe even Mars, if we ever get an atmosphere working over there, and plant some vegetable gardens, and fruit trees. There is plenty of water flying around in the solar system, as comets, and Larry Niven used such an idea in one of his stories that involved terra-forming Mars. Even though it all sounds a bit far out now, there is nothing impossible with God. Who can guess what surprises He has in store for us, the ones who will get to stay with Him,

during His 1000-year long reign? I can
barely wait to find out!

SHOCK

It was one of the scariest dreams I ever experienced. There was a young woman I had been dating for a few months. We had met by chance, and liked each other well enough to see each other a bit longer.

There had been good times, but there had been many troubles, also. She told me one time that I had saved her life. I told her I never saved anyone, but Jesus did.

She had been in a troubled situation when we met, but we got most of that straightened out, and pretty quickly, too, so I know the Lord was helping us. When we first became acquainted, she was not very enthusiastic for the things of the Lord. By the time our pathways diverged again, she was praying a lot of the time, and not just asking for help, but giving thanks more and more. She was reading her Bible, which I gave her, and asking me questions about things that sparked her curiosity, and made her seek understanding. If nothing else came out of the struggle toward maturity that followed, on both our parts, at least she now maintains a closer and closer living relationship with our Lord. Another wonderful and interesting footnote is that she is now married to a really cool guy from Sweden, and, the last I heard, they moved back there sometime in the last two years, though I have not kept in touch. We each have new and different lives, now, and the Lord is blessing everyone involved in one excellent way or another.

At the time this dream happened, we had been around each other for maybe five or six months. I cannot remember the precise time frame, but that is the general area.

It was sometime in the ultra-quiet deep hours of the night, when most humans are oblivious to the happenings upon planet Earth. I would have stayed that way, also, if not for the very realistic and startling thing which woke me right up.

I seemed to hear someone say something, behind my head, as I was sleeping on my left side. I turned toward the voice, expecting to see my girlfriend. Instead, I saw what appeared to be a living skeleton, but with only her long blonde hair, and nothing more. The thing seemed to smile a nasty smile, and started to speak again, and I woke up like a lightning bolt, and sat straight up in bed! I stared at my sleeping girlfriend, slid silently in the blink of an eye out of the bed, and quietly backed out of the room, as I walked up the hall, trying to calm my rattled nerves.

I went into the kitchen, and quietly made myself a cup of coffee. There was no way I was about to go back to sleep any time soon.

I did not tell her anything about the dream, ever. What would be the use? Not much longer after that, within another few months, we each had different things we needed to be doing with our lives and time. Some of the after-effects from that relationship have left me much worse off financially, medically, emotionally, and socially. Whatever parts of it were her fault, I completely forgive. Whatever parts of it were my fault, I hope she will completely forgive. Whatever we each were doing wrongly about any of it, I pray our good Lord will forgive.

I do not understand the full significance of the symbolism in the dream, but a lot of pain and destruction did indeed arrive in my life as a direct result of trying to help someone else have at least some sort of a chance to know a better hope of life. I sort of understood even in the very beginning of it all that maybe the fresh start she needed could be given to her by the Lord, even through someone as insignificant as me. I also somehow understood what it had cost Him to save me, so I hoped I would be tough enough to pay whatever price He needed me to pay to be able to give her a new sunrise in a new land, with Him.

I do hope to meet that married couple on the gold-paved streets someday. It will be good to see those two there, and hear the grand adventures they had with each other and the good Lord, after we lost touch. Come to think of it, there are a lot of folks that I knew in this world that I look forward to meeting again.

I do know that the next time the Lord shows me anyone in my dreams that resembles a living skeleton, I plan to do more than just go into the kitchen, and make a cup of coffee. I plan to quietly exit the house, start my truck, as soon as I can grab the dog, and vanish into the night. I know a freaky dream can follow you anywhere, but I intend not to wait around the blast area, just to see if I can survive another round.

THE CABIN

I was somewhere in the mountains, lost. It was a deadly cold, windy, snow-driven night. I was feeling very little from my elbows outward, and not much feeling left in my legs from the knees down, either. I do not recall seeing the moon, but there was enough light for me to squint my way through the not-quite absolute darkness. The cold had long since penetrated deep into my bones, to the core, and the pain in the marrow was severe. It was like growing pains in the bones, but all over the body at once, and much more extreme. To stay upright, and to move forward, was an agony with each step. The air shocked my lungs and throat, and hurt my sinuses.

As I came around a curve in the natural path the mountainside presented, there was suddenly a square black structure in the night, just about thirty feet ahead. It was a solitary log cabin, with snow blown up along the walls, and covering the roof, but with a stone chimney that poured thick smoke into the night sky! Even though no light shined out from the cabin, I knew that if I could make it there, maybe I could find shelter and warmth. Maybe I would not die tonight, after all.

I fought my way, squeezing out the last of my strength, step by step toward the cabin. The last ten feet were crawling, teeth clenched against the pain, eyes almost frozen shut.

I reached the door, and pushed against it, and managed to get up to my knees, to crawl across the threshold. I used the door frame to pull myself to my feet, willing my hands to grip, though they could no longer feel anything. As I finally was standing, I lurched inside the rest of the way, and slammed the door closed behind me, blinking my eyes against the glare from the fire roaring in the fireplace. The wave of warmth from the fire washed over my face, and a tear would have maybe formed, if the eyelashes had thawed. After a few more seconds, the eyes did warm up and open fully, and as I blinked in the bright firelight, I suddenly noticed a Man sitting on a three-legged stool, just behind where the door opened. He was clothed from head to foot in buckskins, with tough looking fur boots, and some sort of fur hat, also. He also had draped around His shoulders a large fur cloak. He was chewing on a corncob pipe, and leaning back against the wall, where a magnificent, shiny black, flintlock rifle, with bright gold fittings, also leaned against the wall beside Him. As our eyes met, I saw and felt the love and acceptance in Him, for me personally, and I knew it was all right with Him that I came to seek shelter in His warm cabin. He smiled a friendly smile at me, and I felt my shoulders relax with relief.

He told me, without saying a word out loud, to change to some dry clothes He had there for me, and warm up by the fire, and then to eat a little of the hot soup and sandwich He brought to me. I obeyed Him, also without the need to speak. As soon as I finished the soup, and the sandwich, He said, out loud, "Now go over to the bunk, and rest a while. After you are strong again, I have some work I want you to do for Me." Again, I obeyed. As I stretched out on the fur bedclothes, and snuggled in, I looked across the room at Him, and said, "Thank You. I am sorry to be such a trouble." He smiled, as He sat back down on the stool, over by the door. Nothing was going to disturb my rest with Him around.

Sometime later, I woke to find Him up moving around the cabin quietly, organizing things, and packing some things into a small backpack by the door. As I sat up, and stretched, He smiled, and said, "Eat some more for breakfast.

There's coffee, and all the things you like for breakfast, except no pork of any kind. You know I won't feed that poison to people!" He chuckled as He said that.

As I ate, after giving Him thanks, He sat and spoke with me, as He drank His own cup of coffee. It was obvious to me that we had known each other for my whole life, and that He knew everything about me, and still somehow loved and accepted me, in spite of all of it.

I do not recall everything He told me, but I do remember some of the major points, which He somehow made sure to carve deep into my memory. He told me to come inside the shelter, stay inside the shelter, forget about the storm outside, and to sit down at the wooden table, and to WRITE. The last command always has been perceived in my mind as all capital letters, so I guess that's the part where He wanted me to focus most of my effort.

As He stopped by the door, on His way out into the frozen night, He told me the little backpack was for me to take with me when my mission here in the cabin was completed. He told me He would tell me what to write, and how to write it. He told me I would certainly finish my mission, and then leave. As He started to step outside, He turned back and smiled at me one more time, a bright, encouraging, flash of hope in the night, and He said, "Just one more thing. Do NOT give up. I will take care of everything else, but you just keep writing, and do NOT give up!"

Then He pulled the door closed behind Him, and vanished into the storm. I hope I get to see Him again soon. Meanwhile, I must keep writing.

FAMILY REUNION

Without any sort of event leading into the moment, I suddenly found myself flying upwards into a brilliant, clean morning. The sky was blue and gold, with snow white clouds scattered here and there. I found myself flying through a few of the lower clouds on my way up, and I realized that the way I was flying up was by using very strong, enormous wings, like a mighty eagle. The cool air was pure freshness and strength, and the whole world smelled brand new.

I knew where I was going, and why. I was heading toward Jesus, and also all the other family members already there with Him. As I continued climbing effortlessly higher, rejoicing in my limitless strength and endurance, I noticed many bright angels streaking past me toward the Earth below, and also spreading out in every direction, all over the bright morning sky. I could see, in the higher elevations, many people already there, and I saw that I was just one person in a great, upward-flowing river of living saints, all headed up to the Lord.

Another aspect of the order of the people in the stream was that I recognized some people both above me, and also some people below me, and it seemed to my perception that the people below me had each died before I had, but I did not recall the death of any of the people that I recognized which were above me in the flow. It became clear that the further down the stream, the further back in time the person had died. Everyone that was saved was coming to meet the Lord in the air, and the person who was at the very lowest spot in the flow was the man who had died first, Abel. Another strange aspect of our massive group ascent was that everyone seemed to flying upward at a slightly different speed, even though our wings were all about the same size and strength. The people at the lowest places seemed to be climbing the fastest, where as those much closer to the upward end of the stream were flying up much more slowly. The Lord was working each person's rate of ascent so that everyone would arrive together with Him at about the same moment.

The holy prophets and some other special noteworthy heroes of faith were the ones which were already there with Him.

Suddenly, I heard someone call out my name, and I looked down and a little to one side, where I recognized a very dear friend of mine, that had died in 2002. We were delighted to see each other, and steered our flight paths to join together, still always flying steadily up.

Her face lit up even more, and she said, "Look! Here come your parents! And there are mine, too!" Apparently both our sets of parents had already met and joined together on the way up, even though each one of them had died at a different time.

We all had a grand mid-air reunion, and somehow managed to give each other huge, happy bear-hugs, all the time still flying upward. As thrilled as we each were to see one another, and to be actually resurrected and strong, with working wings, we each one still wanted most to complete our ascent, and be with our King. We all, every one of us, had fought to the breaking point to live out our faith for Him, and this was the moment we had all been holding on in hope to live to see. Now, we were finally going to see it, even if most of us had to be raised from our graves be able to participate! Some had been waiting for thousands of years.

The baby, whose name was the last entry in the Book of Life, had not had to wait more than a few minutes after the doctor had spanked breath into that newborn body. If anyone in the delivery room could have understood newborn baby talk, they would have realized that the baby was trying to say the name "Yeshua".

SWORDS IN THE SYNAGOGUES

There had been a time, still in the memories of the grandfathers, when things had been radically different than now. There had been a great peace between the Hebrews and the Greeks, and the Romans had only been a baby nation, but growing stronger day by day. It had been almost a century, but Alexander had once even respected the Hebrew people enough that he not only left their identity intact, and respected their beliefs, but he also did not destroy the land, or enslave or remove them from their homes. There were exceptions, of course, as much as Alexander thought he needed, to suppress rebellion from the Hebrews, during the Greek occupation.

The Greeks had always had their eyes on Israel, ever since Mycenaean times. They had all heard of the events of how

God and Moses had destroyed the mightiest army then in the world, Egypt, and then how Israel had forty years later invaded the land of the giants and absolutely crushed and killed every one of those once-thought-to-be-unconquerable monsters, even in their own fortresses.

In those times, (before Lake Toba in Sumatra had erupted, about 536 A.D.) all of the Promised Land was the richest and most fertile farmland in the entire mid east. After the eruption, permanent climate change reduced the landscape to mostly desert. For thousands of years of history, the Holy Land had been the breadbasket of the world, as well as the primary crossroads. The only exceptions had been in times of severe famine and drought, such as the one which occurred in the days of Joseph.

Even though the Land of Israel was rich, and, for many reasons, much to be desired, only the strongest could ever hold on to it. Alexander wisely decided to rule it more with diplomacy and trade, with a backup plan including military force. His Mycenaean ancestors had attempted to settle there along the coastlands, after God, and Caleb, and Joshua, and the rest of the Hebrew army had utterly exterminated the giants. The Greeks called themselves Philistines, and were a plague for centuries, until God and David finally exterminated not only the very last descendants of the abominations that were the half-breeds, the giants, but also killed or completely drove out all the last traces of the Philistines.

Alexander had understood and respected the Hebrews and their culture enough that he even had 72 Hebrew Rabbis come to Alexandria, and there at the Library of Alexandria, he had them translate the ancient Hebrew scripture into Greek, a massive undertaking which was later known as the Septuagint.

That had been nearly a century ago, and things had degenerated over the decades. Now, the Greeks were openly hostile towards Israel. They launched attacks whenever it suited them, and respected nothing at all about Israel, including God. They had even started to attack deliberately upon the Sabbath, just to try to catch the Hebrews unarmed. They knew that it was not the custom of the Hebrews to wear their weapons to worship. It was considered inappropriate for weapons and things used in war and combat to be worn into the Temple of God on the Sabbath, which was a time to celebrate life and peace, not war and death.

The motivation for these aggressions was multi-faceted. The Romans were now a serious threat to the continued survival of the Greeks. Rome also had a strong trade relationship with the Hebrews, and the Greeks did not want to allow Israel to live in peace and strength, becoming quietly rich and mighty, and standing ready to help the Romans against the Greeks. The Greeks feared the encroachments of a seemingly unstoppable young Rome, and knew that the best place they could ever hope to flee was the Promised Land, which had plenty of food, land, fortified cities, and a lot of people to turn into slaves, once they were subjugated under the Greeks. There were too many Hebrews to take on all at once, so the Greeks had resorted to these hit and run sneak attacks, trying to weaken Israel by means of a long terrible war of attrition against them. The frequency and intensity of the attacks had more than doubled in the last year. The Greeks were feeling the intense pressure from the aggressive Romans, and needed to finish moving the Hebrew obstacle to their relocation out of the way. Another branch of the Mycenaean family tree had pulled the same "run-for-your-life" strategy as the people of Tyre. That had resulted in the founding of Carthage, which would in later years produce Hannibal, so he could go harass the Romans with his elephants.

The latest reports to reach the Hebrews had chilled the hearts of even the toughest of their fighters, and then made them turn into steel, with hard resolve. They already knew the stuff about the men being worked for the rest of their lives as hard-labor slaves, and the women captives being forced into a life of sexual slavery, and the children captives being put to whatever horrible abuse the perverted Greeks could think to do, but the full truth of just how degrading some of those torments had become sickened them all.

The Greeks had in the last few years become famous as the world's first democracy, and also as the world's finest sculptors. No one else produced statues so absolutely flawless in perfect human form, to the smallest detail. The way the

Greeks did it was by pouring plaster around a real human body, after posing and propping it just precisely in the specific pose that was desired by the murderer making the sculpture. The model could not move, even to breathe, for several hours or even days, while the plaster set, as solid as stone. Every one of the models was a dead person, propped in place, smeared with grease all over to help remove the body from the plaster after it dried.

To all of the Hebrews, a sculpture was an abomination, anyway. It made it infinitely worse, now that they knew that the models were all Hebrew captives, stripped naked, and picked over until the Greeks found the one that looked just they way they wanted for the sculpture they were planning. The victim was then suffocated, to kill without leaving wounds or marks upon the body. Many Hebrew captives were killed, just to try to make a sculpture. To add insult, the

Greeks even dressed up their dead victims in Greek war armor and helmets, but often left their bodies shamefully naked. To a Hebrew, man or woman, there could scarcely be a more humiliating death, and then to be left behind, as a stone monument to the stupidity and cruelty of the Greeks, was just too much to contemplate.

It was a shame to an adult Hebrew man to shave off his beard. The Greeks shaved every one of the beards of their victims, after they killed them, so the statue would look Greek. After the final statue mold was finished, it was a simple matter to smooth out the part of the mold for the penis, so the final casting would not appear circumcised. The eyes of the statues were always wide open, because the eyelids open, as rigor mortis sets in.

The face they could not change, though. Not one of the Greek sculptures ever wore a smile. The models for them did not die happy deaths. Even though the men had lost their beards, a close family member, such as a brother, could still easily recognize the face of his own loved one, now turned to bald-faced stone. The way that the news reached Israel was that one of the captives saw his own older brother, made now into a degrading statue, and after he recognized the face, the captive was suddenly filled with not only despair, and overwhelming sadness, but also strengthened by a supernatural rage, and he broke his chains, and killed all of his captors, then changed clothes, and made his way on to a ship headed toward Israel. He had to get word back to let them know what the hellish Greeks were doing here.

Judah Maccabee, and his brother, Jonathan listened silently, with grim faces, as the escaped captive told them his story. When he was done, they went over to him, and each gave him a brief but sincere brotherly hug, and they told him to go rest while they made a new war strategy. They said he could help more, later, after he rested a bit, when they needed more specific details of military intelligence to finalize the details of their new plans. When he left the tent, Judah and Jonathan and the rest of the leaders of Israel discussed how to best counter the Greeks. Many hot-headed notions were tossed about, but wiser strategies prevailed. At the length, Judah stood and told them all that from that point forward, every man, woman, and child of the Hebrews would always be armed, with at least a knife. More intense efforts would be instantly started for each head of a household to train every member of his own family in weapons skills, even the youngest, since any one of them might have to fight for life at a second's notice. When the Sabbaths came, even the highest holy days of the year, and all the feasts and festivals, too, the people would still all wear weapons everywhere they went, whatever they were doing from now on, until the Greeks were dead. Eventually, sometime in the next century, Rome would break the Greeks, but the Hebrews still had to survive for now.

The other immediate component of the new strategy was that a small delegation was dispatched to the Romans, to sign a treaty of alliance against the Greeks. The Roman Senate was happy to join with the Hebrews in this way, since they all hated the Greeks, remembering long years of the Greeks being nasty bullies to everyone around them. Rome was striving for increase, and the biggest barricade to that remained the Greeks. It suited Roman motives well to agree with the Hebrews that if anyone (read Greece) attacked Israel, it would be responded to by Rome as though the offender had attacked Rome personally. The Hebrews, of course, agreed to the same terms, and both sides lived out the agreement in the following years. The Greeks never did destroy Israel, and in time were themselves crushed under the Roman steamroller.

Even though Israel did survive, and grow much stronger over time, nothing could match the steroid-like growth of Rome, and, ironically, less than two centuries later, Rome ruled heavily over Israel.

Perhaps even more ironically, within another century after that, the Greeks were once again major players in the story of the Hebrew people, since many Greeks were people that now worshipped the King of Israel, and obeyed Him as their own King, and loved Him enough to willingly suffer and even die to honor Him, even if He was just a Hebrew. Two more centuries later, and Rome itself had been conquered by the King of the Hebrews.

SIX POUNDS OF LIGHT, TO GO

No one is absolutely certain precisely who first discovered it, or just how such a discovery was obtained. At some point in the past, somebody in an operating room noticed that the weight of a human body changes at the very moment of death.

This might be dismissed as bad science, or improper weighing techniques, but the fact has been observed many, many times, and does indeed occur, for each and every human at the time of their departure. There is no valid physical reason for this effect.

The only logical conclusion is that a person's soul weighs about six pounds. It does not seem to make any difference as to the physical size of the person, or the sex, or the age, or the medical condition just prior to death.

This has caused much speculation, and some heated debate, amongst the folks who know this fact, but cannot explain it. Cynical-minded doctors refuse to believe that it really happens, even when their own instruments confirm it. Religious fanatics claim rightly that it is one of the mysteries of God, but also claim wrongly that science does not know anything about truth at all.

It is well known from the work of Einstein and others that light is strongly affected by gravity. Whereas light is usually regarded as having no mass, and therefore should have no weight, and should not be affected by gravity, the scientific observations have proven that that is not the case.

Even though light is affected by gravity, no one has yet managed to actually weigh a beam of light. Whatever the weight of light turns out to be, it does not seem to weigh very much. Light proves itself to be fast enough, strong enough, and light-weight enough so that only the most extreme conditions can actually stop a light beam, using only gravity. Mathematics, as well as observation, has confirmed that the things known as black holes do actually exist, and are actually to be found at the center of every galaxy in the sky. Thus, it is proven that light is not immune to gravity.

For a small bundle of light to be able to weigh about six pounds would require the light to either be actually a different sort of ultra-heavy, concentrated light, or to contain something in addition to ordinary light, from beyond the electromagnetic spectrum.

Just as no one has managed to weigh a single beam of light, even so, no one has ever managed to weigh a human soul. The only person Who could ever do anything like that is God.

No one has yet been able to directly observe the soul's departure, or to film it as it occurs. No one can tell whether the particular soul leaves the body in an upward direction, or a downward direction.

All we can conclude, for certain, is that about six pounds leaves the physical body at the moment of death. If it is composed of light, it must be extraordinarily concentrated, to be dense enough for human scales to record the effect.

Perhaps the closest equivalent event in the physical structure of creation is when a star dies, and goes supernova. A mind-numbing explosion of energy release occurs, and the dying star ejects, at near light-speed, very much solid material, or gas and plasma, anyway, as well as enough light to momentarily outshine everything in the radius of thousands of light years.

The dying person may also produce something on the order of a supernova, but in a frequency and spectrum that humanity does not even realize does actually exist. Perhaps the electromagnetic spectrum extends far beyond the limits we currently perceive.

We only have one recorded event in the history of the world in which human observers actually saw a living Spirit. When Jesus was baptized, both our good Lord, and also John the Baptist, his cousin, actually saw the Holy Spirit of Almighty God descend from Heaven, like a dove, and indwell, and remain upon Jesus. I must admit a strong curiosity as to whether or not Jesus immediately gained another six pounds of weight. It also makes me wonder if when He said "Paid in full!" and gave up the Ghost, did His physical body lose six pounds, or twelve?

God is Light, and in Him is no darkness at all. We are made in His image. We are also built of light.

Whenever the time is right, according to His calendar, and wristwatch, I

respectfully request that I will be given
six pounds of light, to go, please.

WITHOUT THE VEIL

It happened near the end of the year, back in 1974. I was still in the Navy, and our ship was docked in South Korea.

I was out at night, in full uniform. There were two of us making all our appointed rounds as Shore Patrol officers.

We went into one of the more busy bars, and headed up the stairs. We were required to at least make an official appearance at every bar open along our assigned route.

As was usual, once we entered the top floor room, the bartender girl said," Shore Patrol!" She said it with a big smile, but in a loud enough voice so everyone in the bar could be warned, and not let us catch them doing anything for which we would have to arrest them. She also filled a couple of glasses with 7-Up, and shoved them across the bar at us with a wink. She knew better than to try to give us alcohol.

We accepted the drinks, which was perfectly fine, and normal custom. After all, we were out on patrol for four straight hours, always moving along, from bar to bar, and we became thirsty, just as anyone would.

As I took a small sip from my glass, my peripheral vision noticed someone approaching from my left side. My patrol partner was standing on my right side. I placed the glass back on the bar, and turned slightly to see clearly just who had arrived.

At first glance, the person appeared to be just another woman in the bar, looking very much like everyone else who was there. It was not until she opened her mouth, and began to speak in Korean, to the bartender girl, who also answered her in Korean. The new arrival was standing only about two feet away from me. As she began speaking, suddenly, the entire environment shifted to another perspective. Although her outer appearance did not change one bit, somehow, I perceived that what I was seeing was someone inhabited by a very malevolent spirit, and the overall impression was like watching a life-sized wooden ventriloquist's dummy. The mouth and eyes moved and blinked, and did more or less normal conversational things, but there was clearly someone else inside the poor person, manually moving her face and body to do whatever little evils she was force-marched to perform.

I had not had a drink of alcohol, or anything intoxicating, for over five months. I was trying to behave much more seriously and sincerely as a Christian gentleman should behave, and had stayed away from anything that impeded my walk with the Lord.

I felt goose bumps, and a shiver of fear shot down my spine, and tightened up my gut. My jaws also tightened, and I did not know if in the next few seconds, we might be under violent attack. As it happened, the beast turned and walked away, after about four or five minutes. I was still watching it walk away, and yet, very ready to run full speed right out the door.

A couple of minutes later, my partner finished his drink, and asked me if I was ready. I nodded yes, still watching the strange thing closely. He said that he would just take a minute to inspect the men's room, so to speak. While he did so, I remained just where I was, still staring at the dangerous abomination, which had never once looked directly into my eyes, or spoken a word directly to me. It went over to a booth in the room, and sat down with two other people.

In a moment, my partner returned, and said, "Okay." As we moved toward the door, I made sure to keep my eye locked upon the threat, and sort of backed out of the door as we left.

As we went down the stairs, to move to the next bar down the street, another cold shiver went racing along my spine. I wondered what, if anything, I should do about the thing I had just seen. I did not mention it to my partner, except to ask if he noticed anything unusual about the woman. He said that he had barely even noticed her.

I know it could not have actually hurt us, not with the Son of God standing watch over our lives. I am very sure that the thing could see several good angels standing near us, with flaming swords drawn and ready. I did not see the good angels, but I know that they were with us.

I know what I saw. I think it was just trying to mess with my head, and trouble my heart. Although it was indeed disturbing, no lasting damage was done, even though I still feel a memory of that cold shiver, as I first perceived the thing standing next to me. I wonder what ever happened to that poor lady. I have thought about her, and prayed for her throughout all these thirty five years since that night. I know the good Lord can help her, but there was truly nothing I could do for her, except pray.

I hope no one else has experiences like that one. That's the sort of thing from which nightmares are made. I also hope every Christian will realize that these things are very real indeed. Trust the Lord to protect us, but pray for those hopeless wretches held captive in such bondage.

IN MEMORY OF CHESTER GILLIAM

Sometimes, the finest moments in a person's life are the last few seconds before they graduate to Heaven. Perhaps they have lived a good and productive life, or perhaps otherwise, but every once in a while, a hero appears, right out of the wood work, and does the thing needed to be done, regardless of personal cost.

The world is very familiar with the story of Todd Beamer, and the great heroes with him, that overpowered the high-jackers, and saved either the Capitol Building, or the Whitehouse. They knew that the plane they were riding in had to be crashed, but they must not dare let the murderers do it their evil way. So, they made a quick plan, born in desperation, and saved a whole lot of innocent people on the ground. Certainly it cost all of those heroes more pain, and a sooner death, but they did the impossible, by paying the price of the sacrifice, with their lives.

Another man of similar character, and nobility, was named Chester Gilliam. He was eighty two years old when he decided to go to see a monster truck race. It was the precise sort of thing any boy would love to see, no matter how many years he had been alive. Chester was still very strong, especially for 82, and got around very well.

The whole event was very exciting, as such things always are, and everyone in the crowd was cheering and yelling for their favorite driver, most often by the name of the truck! The great machines were all roaring like savage beasts, and leaping all around the arena like hungry dinosaurs. Things were happening so fast that the announcer could not keep up with all of the action.

Suddenly it happened! A part in the steering controls of one of the monster trucks snapped, and the unstoppable five ton machine, like a fast freight train off of the tracks, veered sharply, and headed right for the stands where Chester and some other folks were sitting. Some of the people jumped up and sprang to get clear, but some were frozen in terror. Chester saw immediately what was about to happen, and knew his old legs would not move that fast, but he reached out, and grabbed a 10 year old boy that was sitting nearby, and he threw the boy clear of the crash, less than two seconds before the truck rammed into the stands, immediately killing Chester!

Someone in the crowd, on the opposite side of the arena, had been filming the whole thing with a video cam. The network news showed the tragic, yet spectacularly heroic episode, the next day. It was only a brief film clip, just about five seconds long, but it was clear to see the boy flying through the air to safety, and Chester Gilliam's long, strong, mighty old arms launching the child out of death, and into life. The clip was so brief, that they played it twice. Fortunately, the angle of the shot made it so that the truck itself obscured the actual impact sight.

It's strange to think of the most important and mighty moments in a man's life to be somehow reserved for the last few seconds, after 82 long years. What is wonderful is how the Lord told the man to save the child, and instantly gave him the extra strength and speed he needed. In this case, the Lord did not have to send one of His angels do it. He had one of His men do it, instead!

THE MOUNTAIN

The three men shared looks of sudden surprise, and curiosity, as they noticed that the entire landscape around them had instantly changed radically from the familiar hills around Galilee. The view was much grander, and far more severe, with a stark and savage character. There was still vegetation, but far less than the abundance of Israel, as they knew it. There were rugged mountains, including the one upon which they were climbing, at this moment. A few seconds earlier, it had just been another green hillside in Israel.

The disciples had seen the Lord do something like this miracle once before, when they had all been out on the Sea of Galilee, and the Lord had suddenly transported the entire ship, along with all of them on board, straight to the landing where they were headed, despite the tough headwind. It had occurred both times in the blink of an eye.

When the disciples had been finishing breakfast this morning, back in town, Jesus had walked in, and picked Peter, James, and John to follow Him out of town. Now they were still following Him, struggling up the steep slopes of Jabel-el-Laws, the Mountain of God's Word. It was many miles south of Jerusalem, in Midian. It was the same mountain upon which Moses had first met the Lord, and later received the Two Tablets. It was also the same mountain where Elijah had fled, after defeating the prophets of the enemy, upon Mount Carmel. The name by which the Hebrews called this mountain was Mount Horeb. Moses had asked the Lord to reveal Himself, so Moses could see Him, and God had him stand in the mouth of a cave in Jabel-el-Laws, while He passed by Moses, and covered his eyes until He was past, so Moses only saw the Lord from the back, and not His Face, for His Glory was too great for Moses to bear. Elijah had run there to hide, after a meal of angel's food, so he could make the whole forty day journey at once. The Lord had called Elijah to come out to the mouth of the same cave where Moses had stood many centuries earlier, and the Lord spoke then with Elijah, Person-to-person. God did not speak in the mighty storm that came first, or in the fire that came next, or in the earthquake after that. God spoke in a still, small Voice, reminding Elijah to be still, and know that God is God.

The disciples were watching their footing, and looked up when they suddenly saw a very bright light shine down on them from higher up the mountainside. As they blinked and squinted, they could make out three men standing together talking. They were discussing something about how Jesus was going to finally accomplish His eternal mission, and kill sin and evil, once, and for all.

Even though the disciples had never seen a picture of either Moses or Elijah, they all immediately knew precisely the identity of each man. Jesus looked very different, however, and was actually glowing everywhere, from head to toe, even brighter than the sun. It was very difficult to look in His direction, and not want to cover one's eyes.

Peter rashly blurted out that it was a delight for the disciples to be there, and would the Lord like the men to hastily build three temples, one for Jesus, one for Moses, and one for Elijah? Peter's ignorant comment only happened because he was not yet born again of the Holy Spirit, and could not understand the things of God, yet. Even so, his words reveal a lingering problem with many Hebrews, even to this day. Until each person is born again of the Holy Spirit, the Jews tend to reverence Moses and

Elijah even more than they do reverence Jesus, the Person that actually is the rightful and Holy King of Israel.

Well, the Heavenly Father was not about to tolerate such a blasphemous statement, even done in ignorance, even from Peter. He immediately spoke up, and told them that JESUS was His Son, the Beloved One, and they were to obey JESUS!

As soon as the men heard God's Voice, they fell in terror to the ground, and remained there quivering in fear, until Jesus walked over, reached down, and lifted each of them up to his feet again. Jesus instructed the men to tell the vision to no one, until the Son of Man was raised from the dead. This added to their confusion, but, after just hearing the Voice of Almighty God command them to listen to Jesus, and obey Him, they were not about to argue. They all walked back down the mountainside, which suddenly became a small green hillside in

Israel once again. Peter and James heard a small yelp of a muffled laugh from John, the youngest one, and the last one in the line of the four of them walking back down the hill. As Peter and James looked back over their shoulders, to see what John was amused by, John reached out, and picked a few snowflakes off of James' shoulder, and held it there to show them. It had been snowing up on Jabel-el-Laws, but it was warm and spring-like here. The vision had been much more real than they had thought!

ELIJAH THE BAPTIST

Two of the tree tasks had to remain unfinished. The sudden departure by means of a chariot drawn by horses of fire had been ordered before the anointing of the kings could be achieved.

Right after Elijah had been used by the Lord to defeat the prophets of Baal (over 400 of them) he had suddenly been gripped by unreasonable fear, and fled unnecessarily from the threats of Jezebel. He thought that he was the only person left in all of Israel that still loved the God of Abraham, Isaac, and Jacob. After demonstrating so much stunning faith and courage before all the nation of Israel, in which he had actually challenged them to either serve God, or serve the devil, and go to hell, if they did, he then was found by God hiding deep within a cave in the side of a cliff, fearing for his life.

God had made him come to the door of the cave, and, in a still, small Voice, told him three assignments he was to complete. God ordered Elijah to anoint Elisha the Tishbite to become the next holy prophet of God unto Israel. This first task Elijah did indeed accomplish, not long after, and the two prophets spent quite some time together before Elijah was taken up to Heaven.

God also commanded Elijah to anoint the next king of Israel, and also the next king of Syria. As events of war and turmoil continued to develop both within, and all around Israel, and in other nations, including Syria, the two prophets were called off on other needed assignments, and as far as we can discern from Scripture, Elijah never did actually complete the specified anointing of the two kings. He was also foretold to turn the hearts of the people back to their God, which he did. After the defeat of the prophets of Baal, the people of Israel began to seriously repent of their wickedness, and turn back to God. As their improvement continued, God removed both Ahab, and also Jezebel, which had been the mortal enemies of Elijah. Ahab died from wounds in battle, after behaving in a cowardly manner, dressing in an ordinary soldier's uniform instead of wearing the king's armor, like he persuaded brave King Josiah, King of Judah, to do. Ahab's hope was that all of the enemy would focus on Josiah, and leave his own sorry hide alone. They did just that, too, but God protected good King Josiah, and somehow an enemy arrow found its' way into King Ahab's leg, which caused a deep wound, and he bled to death even as he was being driven in a panic from the battlefield in his chariot. Ahab was always more of a scumbag than a king, even on the day he died. Men loyal to God obeyed Elijah and threw Jezebel down from the 90-foot-tall tower of Jerusalem, and the dogs ate her bones outside the city walls, just as foretold.

The Lord Jesus told us that the spirit of Elijah was upon John the Baptist, and that John, as had been Elijah, was sent to turn the hearts of the people back to their God. Elijah himself had certainly succeeded in his mission to confront, and recall Israel to God. John the Baptist also certainly succeeded in his own mission to turn the hearts of Israel back to their God, in preparation for the arrival of the King of Israel. Even though John did not actually crown Jesus, yet, with a solid gold crown (made to resemble thorn branches woven into a crude mockery of a crown), John did crown Jesus with the very first confession of just Who Jesus is, when John declared Jesus as the Lamb of God, which takes away the sin of the world. This is the reason why John the Baptist is called the greatest of all men, second to Jesus, because John is the very first human to ever say "There is the Son of God!" At any rate, John is the very first human to ever say that about the real Son of God.

At that time, God the Father also crowned Jesus with the Holy Spirit, and declared over Him, "You are My Only Begotten Son, and You please Me very much, indeed!"

So, even though re-incarnation is not taught in the Word of God, since it appointed once unto man to live, and once to die, and after that, the judgment, we do see some unusual cases where the particular "spirit of a man" is somehow applied unto another man further downstream in time. This is not some sort of haunting, or demonic possession, but a sharing of gifts and abilities, and even more so, priorities, and understandings, of deep, deep Godly wisdom. It is like an inheritance from a father to a son, as with material things, but in these cases, it applies to spiritual gifts. Since every good and perfect gift comes down from the Father of Lights, in Whom there is no variableness, or shadow of turning, God does not remove the ability from one person, but the person themselves may cause it to wither away into uselessness, if the gift is unexercised, or malnourished.

Elisha asked of Elijah that he would grant him to have a double portion of Elijah's spirit, after he left. Elijah said it was a hard thing to do, but it would be so, if Elisha saw Elijah taken up into Heaven. A short time later those events occurred. Elisha went on to work twice as many miracles as had Elijah.

So, was John the Baptist actually Elijah, re-incarnated? Absolutely not! But he did fulfill all the roles ascribed unto Elijah in the ancient prophecies, at least for the first arrival of the King. It had to be done that way, because the next time the King will arrive will be after the tribulation, at the seventh trumpet, just before everything on Earth freezes to death forever in the total darkness. Elijah will have been here again in the flesh, not resurrected, not re-incarnated, but carried back from Heaven in the same chariot drawn by horses of living fire that carried him up there centuries ago. Enoch will be there with Elijah, as they challenge the whole world, one last time, to forsake evil, and humbly bow before the Son of God.

There will certainly come forth a Day in which every knee will bow, and every tongue confess that Jesus is God. God has said so in His word, and His word is Truth, and God and His word are One, and His word does not return unto Him void, and the Scripture cannot be broken!

HAPPY ENDINGS

Sometimes it seems to me, and I am pretty sure also to you, that we are spending a whole lot of effort, money, and time trying to do a few worthwhile good deeds in our lifetimes. Often I have noticed that for someone else to have mercy, I myself have to make a sacrifice. If the person has offended me, then I must give up my righteous indignation (how DARE they?!), as well as my desire for revenge, and give place to wrath, since the wrath of man works not the righteousness of God. I have to release the anger unto the Lord, and keep on releasing it, every time it comes back to haunt and harass me again. Of course, this is the Lord's express commandment, and, since we love Him, we obey Him.

The extra mile step in the commandment is much harder, though. I am required to even pray sincerely for the person, or persons, and wish them healing and restoration unto our Lord. This has always proven to be the most difficult part of my walk trying to follow the leadership of Jesus, and He blazes a very rough, tough-going, off-road type path through the middle of the wilderness, every time. Trying to understand His lead, and follow it accurately, is a real challenge, even for the most dedicated and sincere of Christians. I know, because over the course of almost sixty years in this world, I have actually met and known a few truly sincere Christians. They have all assured me that the walk following Jesus is the very hardest trail in the world to walk. After several decades of trying, I must agree.

More than once in these years and in the course of these adventures, it has seemed as if every single attempt to do goodness was either met with no result, or a backlash, or betrayal, instead of a good result. These feelings eventually pass, and, even if they do not, I still have to forgive them! Man alive, talk about a tough assignment!

So, that is why it was an overwhelming joy, and a stunning surprise, when I was just channel surfing on the television a couple of weeks ago, and I happened to stop on the local broadcast of "Life Today" hosted by James Robinson, and, since it was Wednesday night, it was the regular weekly "Wednesdays With Beth" featuring guest teacher Beth Moore. I admire Beth's special teaching gift. She has a talent for being able to find practical applications from the Word of God in ways to effectively walk out our lives following Him. She is especially insightful about our individual relationship with our Heavenly Father.

The surprise part was that in the audience, behind Beth Moore, as she spoke to a small group of about fifty or sixty women in the small studio, (ladies that were there to study the Word of God, with Beth Moore, as their special tutor) sat a very familiar person. Suddenly there was the face of a young lady I had known many years before. We had dated for a little less than two years. When I had known her, she was, at best, a very casual believer. She had been hurt in the early and middle years of her life, and had been taken advantage of, by, especially, her own family, and the scars ran deep, and had never fully healed.

Despite all of that, she had been close to God as a little girl, and had never fully ceased to believe. When I saw her in the audience, behind Beth Moore, she was wearing her glasses, taking notes diligently, and listening intently, to every thing Beth said. That lady was obviously very, very serious about learning everything she could about Jesus, and how to walk faithfully, and peacefully, with Him, from now on!

I wish maybe I could take some small credit for that wonderful transformation and healing that I saw had been accomplished in her, but I surely cannot. We were not in contact for the last three or four years, ever since I learned that she had met and married a fine fellow from Sweden. During the time I had known her, I had tried to witness to her about the Lord, and tried to live it out sincerely, too. At one point, when an especially beloved cat, named KK, which she had given me six years earlier, had suddenly passed away, she commented that she knew, even though I was in much sadness over the loss of our friend, I would still always keep on having faith in the Lord. At those times, even though she did not place much faith in the Lord, she was certain that I did.

When I saw her that day, studying the Word of God, and loving doing it, too, I knew the Lord had answered all of my prayers for her. I now am certain that my life was of at least some value to the Kingdom of Heaven, or else the King of Heaven would never have arranged for me to see that my friend's story had a happy ending. I am looking forward to someday meeting them all, including her husband, her brother, and sisters, and her dad and mom, and all of them, in a second life in the world to come. You see, I also prayed for them, too, and the Lord does answer a well-meaning, sincere prayer, even if He sometimes takes a few years to do it.

THE DEEPEST CUT

The Lord said that He would cut a line in the Earth, with His Holy Sword (which is His Holy Word), and that He would set on one side of the line those that delighted in righteousness, and loved doing good, and giving unselfishly, and stayed true to His Way, and followed Him. On the other side of the line, He would set those that delighted in doing evil, and disregarded righteousness, and lived self-centered lives of greed and falsehood.

We often can notice, since the same Almighty God made both the physical aspects of Creation, and also the spiritual aspects of Reality, seen and unseen, that there are many parallels between the physical and the spiritual. One of the least advertised phenomena in astrophysics is the "Mercator" projection-type map of all the total luminous matter in the Universe. In that, the whole sphere of the sky is compressed into a large, wide oval map representation. Right in the central area of the map, the density patterns of the stars and galaxies are concentrated to form a likeness of a gigantic Man, as tall as the whole Sky! He seems to be in mid-stride, as though taking a step forward toward the observer! The proportions of the image pattern are perfect in respect to average human proportions. The image is not detailed, being comprised of many small dots of the bright points in the Sky, but it is unmistakable in its' eerie resemblance to a Man in the Sky.

There is also a physical parallel to the deep cut the Lord declared in the Earth. Running from north to south, a great split divides one side of the Middle East from the other. Farther south, it also splits a large section of Africa, where it is known as the Great Rift. North of Africa, it runs through part of the Red Sea, in particular, the Gulf of Aquba, and (except for the narrow, raised portion that crosses from west to east about the halfway mark of the deep Gulf, which was the escape bridge of Moses and the children of Israel, after the Lord blew the waters away for a while) the entire thing is so deep and wide that it rivals the Grand Canyon in depth and distance.

As it passes through the Holy Land, it is the deep floor of the Dead Sea, and the Sea of Galilee, and the Jordan River runs along the top of it. It is the deepest cut in the crust of the Earth.

I suppose the main point that such a correspondence suggests is that indeed, the same Voice which declared a deep cut in the spiritual realm in the Earth, also showed us that He can declare a very deep cut in the physical Earth, too, just to prove to us, that, if He says it, He will do it. That seems to provide yet more evidence to the absolute reality of His Holy Word, as well as His Holy Power, and also, His Absolute Authority. If the deepest cut in the Earth is not convincing enough, perhaps the fact that He painted His Image with the light of the stars and galaxies, and made it almost to scale (as tall as the whole of Creation) might be persuasive. If He had made His Self-portrait to true scale, it would have been so big, that we never could have seen it. Even the physical parallel is so huge that we could not see it without modern telescopes, so the secret was hidden until these last days. Who can guess what amazing wonders He still has stored up, with which to delight us?

THE BROKEN CUP

If you suggest to a Jewish person that the broken cup (or glass) represents the broken Temple in Jerusalem, they will agree with you, and perhaps wonder why a gentile would even notice such a thing. It is tradition that the groom in a Jewish wedding stomps a glass to pieces, as part of every Jewish wedding. This is to remember the lost, crushed Temple in Jerusalem, which was broken down by the Romans in 70 A.D.

But if you mention to them that this perfectly illustrates the principle that Jesus taught, to make clean the inside of the cup, and then the whole cup was clean, they likely would not know what you are talking about, unless they are also our Christian brother, or sister. If you also tell them that the same concept applies in the example the Lord gave of placing new wine only in new wine skins, they might politely listen, but not yet see it.

They are well aware of the story of Judah Maccabee (meaning "hammer") and his brother Jonathon, the great resistance generals of the people of Israel, which fought off the oppression of the Syrians, until Judah was killed in battle, but Jonathon carried on, and eventually the day came when the priests of Israel were able to go into the Temple again. They know that the first thing the priests did was to completely purify the Temple, and re-dedicate it to God. This is the historical event, around 162 B.C., which is the meaning behind Chanukah, when only one day's worth of lamp oil kept the menorah lit for a whole eight days.

When an object of utility value, such as a cup, became contaminated, there were provisions ordered by God, in the law, to clean the thing, and make it fit for use again. This is the cleaning of the inside, to make the whole thing of value, once more. There were, however, some contaminations that God did not want cleaned up, but destroyed. Groves, and high places, which were set up in rebellion against God, and used for perverted worship of demons, were never to be used again, but were to be absolutely broken, and the pieces burned. This even included the killing of the priests of the devil, and the burning of their bones upon their own evil altars, followed by the total destruction of those altars. The ashes were to be forgotten, blown away by the clean wind that God sent afterward.

When Jesus spoke about contamination, He defined it as something that proceeds from the inside to the outside, from the evil in the heart. He said that nothing which enters a man from the outside can possibly defile him, but only those things which proceed from the inside out. He said that we are made clean by the Word which He spoke to us, and that we purify ourselves by obeying the Truth. He said that one that was already clean did not need to wash again, except for his dirty feet. As the Holy Spirit cleans the inside of the heart, soul, and mind of the reborn, and the believer follows the lead of the Holy Spirit, purifying himself by obeying the Truth, the only parts which remain to be cleaned are the dirty parts of the believer, the interaction with the fallen world of these times. We can "wash our feet" by walking more in the clean things of God, and less in the dirty things of the world.

It has been suggested by some preachers that we should guard our thought life. I think that is a wise suggestion. The only trouble with that is that no one can do it. Thoughts are like the fleeting signals on a scanner, here a moment, then gone, and they seem to come from somewhere else beside our own minds, at times. The only effective way to "guard our thoughts" is to set our hearts upon the Kingdom of God, and His Righteousness, and then all things will be added unto us. The Lord declares that a man's heart devises his way, but the Lord directs his steps. Keep on re-setting your heart upon the Lord, and His Way, and obey Him, and He will set your thoughts in order for you, eventually, and, in the meantime, He will stay right there with you until the confusion is over, and the fear fades away.

When the temple was cleaned in 162 B.C., it was the proper thing to do with it, since the contamination had come from the outside in, in the form of the defiling Syrians. When the Temple was broken, and destroyed, in 70 A.D., it was the proper thing to do with it, since the contamination had indeed materialized from the inside out this time, as the high priests had worshipped the devil, and murdered the Holy Begotten Son of God. Once the cup, the Temple, had been defiled in such a way, from the inside out, it could only be destroyed, not ever cleaned enough to remove that horrible evil done in it, by its' own high priests. Openly rebellious warfare, and even murder, against the Holy Son of God, is not something that the Father of Jesus is ever going to let rest, un-avenged!

Nevertheless, the God of Abraham, Isaac, and Jacob, is first, always, a God of Justice, then, also, a God of Mercy. If it were not so, there never would have been sent any Messiah. Our Messiah, Jesus, did indeed bring Mercy, but He could only do it justly after first fulfilling Justice, which demanded the death penalty for our sins. God, as Father, poured out His vengeance and fulfilled His Justice, with the obedient help of Jesus, and we were spared the death penalty that every one but Jesus actually deserves.

That is why it is appointed once unto man to live, and once to die, and after that, the Judgment. We live in

contaminated vessels, since the evil came
not only into our lives from the outside,
but also came out of our lives into the
world, to hurt others. Not one of us,
including me, can truthfully say that we
never hurt anyone else, at least their
feelings, in an undeserved way. The only
human Who ever made it through this
world, without doing that, died on the
cross that was reserved for each of the
rest of us, so that He might reserve us for
Himself.

EPI-GENOME

A very strange and unexpected thing was noticed one day. Scientists noted that in some sets of identical twins, both with identical DNA, even given the very same environment, upon rare occasions, one twin developed a particular disease, and the other twin did not. Scientists could not unravel that mystery, until further intense research into the problem revealed the existence of a secondary regulating agent, in addition to the actual genetic code structure. They named this strange new structure the "epi-genome", which describes its' parallel, yet entirely different function in comparison to the DNA strands.

In a very small nutshell, what the epi-genome does is activate, or deactivate, individual, and sets, and groups of genes, in the DNA, which manifests in various types of tissue formation, structure, repair, and normal (or abnormal) functionality. It turns certain genes on, or off.

Another difference is that the epi-genome does not seem to be nearly as rugged as the actual DNA, which can withstand even some measure of radiation, chemical damage, free radicals, and other types of physical assaults, and still survive intact, or be repaired once more. Environmental variables, such as chemicals, radiation, smoking, alcohol, stress, and other sorts of trauma can do more intense, and longer lasting, damage to the epi-genome than to the genome.

As can easily be observed in many other things the good Lord has designed, and created, perhaps there are some points of congruence between the DNA vs. epi-genome structure, and the structure of the human heart, when surrounded and filled with good, or evil. The human heart was designed and created by a good God, and made and shaped in His Own Image, in likeness to His heart, and so we can love, create, build, plan good things, do good things, and live decent lives, giving goodness to others. Those things are the precise things which were designed and built, and hard-wired, into our hearts way back in the Garden of Eden. Things have changed since the original design was built.

When the spirit in a person's heart is wicked, and rejoices to do evil, then the person's life is warped, and ruined, as the distorting influence of the self-centered and proud-hearted attitudes poison every aspect of the person and their entire life, tainting every deed with self-interest, and short circuiting every motive with lust for personal gain or vainglory. This is the natural state of every person born into this world, ever since the Garden of Eden, except one special Person, Jesus Christ. Since Jesus is the direct DNA descendant of Holy Almighty God, Jesus is the only Person since the Garden to be born with pure, clean spiritual DNA. In fact, since neither Adam, nor Eve was ever born, because each one was uniquely created, Jesus Christ is the only human being ever born, that started out His life being born into this world completely Holy, clean, and free of sin in any way. That is why He was the only human who ever lived that could fully pay the just penalty for sin, which, for all the rest of us, the sinful ones, would have been that same death, naked, upon a cross.

When a person is saved by the Lord, which is a freely given gift from Him, if He chooses you to be one of the ones to whom He wishes to give it, then a new spirit is born into the person's heart, and the person then begins to start to understand some of the mysteries of God. The natural man cannot understand the things of God, but the re-born man can, and will, with time, study, prayer, and most of all, the grace of the good Lord to understand more.

The Lord has declared that it is from the heart that good things come forth, and it is from the heart that evil things come forth. Man, without Jesus, is doomed to have an evil heart, until the Holy Spirit in the heart of the new believer turns the tide of the thoughts, words, and deeds of the person, from the inside out, by positive leadership, and not forced coercion. As the attitudes in the heart and mind change, the words and deeds soon follow. People do what they basically want to do, if they can. If they love the Lord, with re-born hearts, they want to hear, and obey, His instructions. The Lord told us that those who love Him do the things He commands.

So, a re-born spirit heals, and restores, the old wicked heart, to love to do goodness, instead of evil. As the epi-genome can either distort, or correctly regulate, the DNA, so the Spirit will restore, and regulate, the heart, the mind, the soul, and the strength of the believer. The only choice the believer is given is whether or not to obey. Belief is not a choice, but obedience is.

A PITCHER OF WATER

He told them to go into the village, and there they would meet a man carrying a pitcher of water. They were ordered to follow him, and when they arrived at the house where he was carrying the water, they were to ask the owner of the house, "The Master says, 'Where is the room where I may keep My Passover with My disciples?'" As soon as they did this, the man smiled, and quickly led them inside, down a hall, across a courtyard, into another part of the large house, near the back, and up stairs into a very large upper room, usually reserved for important family guests from out of town. Usually, the room was occupied during the week of Passover, but things had worked out differently this year, and the room was available immediately, for the use of the King. The two disciples prepared, with the generous help and supply of the homeowner, everything they would later need for the supper.

It seems to be a continuation of theme in the mind of Jesus, to use the symbolism of the pitcher of water. If the Holy Spirit is the Living Water, then supposedly, Jesus is the Living Pitcher, full of Living Water, which He carried from the Father, to share with the rest of us.

In parallel concept, each re-born believer is also a newly filled pitcher, also full of Living Water. How appropriate that the very first miracle recorded in John involves water containers, empty to start, that Jesus commanded to be filled with pure water, and then He miraculously changed the water to excellent wine!

In another parable, He teaches us that new wine must be put into new wineskins, in order to preserve both. A re-born believer will, given time, and having sincerity in his heart, begin to live a new, healed, and positively productive life. The new wine, along with the new wineskin (the believer), both age well together over time, and co-exist peacefully, working together for mutual goals. Respect, affection, loyalty, and understanding increase over years, as the person is matured in their faith.

In another case, Mary broke a flask of oil, and anointed the feet of Jesus. In some cases, the believer must be willing to cheerfully have his own human life, including wishes, dreams, plans, fortunes, opportunities, relationships, careers, and all manner of the stuff of life, be allowed to be broken into pieces also. Sometimes that is the only way in which the blessing inside can be given out to the world as a testimony for the Lord.

So, from the very beginning of His Ministry in this world, and all the way through it, and up to the very end, He continued to draw our attention to the precious treasure inside, shifting focus away from external things, toward the internal. No matter how good any person looks on the outside, they must not forget that Jesus is looking deeply into their heart. Beauty and goodness within the heart cannot be hidden, and neither can be ugliness, or evil.

BIG SNOW

The good Lord has blessed me to live in this wonderful old home for fifty three years. I still have the same little bedroom that my parents gave me when I was a little five year old boy. It has been a singular privilege to experience this almost unheard-of blessing, and I cannot think of anyone else that I ever met who was blessed in such a way.

Today was the strangest of days, in many ways. It began with a light snow dusting overnight, but the snowfall continued all through the day, and into the night, setting new records for single day snowfall totals. The flakes were huge, as big as silver dollars at times, and it fell straight down, with almost no wind to stir it or whirl it into drifts. It left a nice, thick beautiful layer of frosting all over everything. It was a wet, sticky snow, and all of the hedges in front of my house bent over from the heavy weight of it.

I am very glad that I was allowed to stay here this long, and to witness this unique event, a mammoth snowstorm, but without wind, right here in Dallas County. I spent the whole wonderful and mysterious day just like many other folks in our land these days, namely, fighting to save my home from impending foreclosure. It is a day with many memories burned into my mind, and my heart, which will not be forgotten soon.

I know the good Lord gave me this home for all of these blessed years, and I also know that it actually still belongs to Him, and I also belong to Him: lock, stock, and barrel. If He decides to allow me to stay, then I will try to live here as I am told to do in His Scripture, and as I am led to do by His Spirit, but I have already confessed to Him that I know I will not always get it right. I have already asked Him to forgive not only whatever I have done in the past, or am doing right now, even the things I do not realize, but to also perhaps somehow forgive whatever mistakes I might still make in the future. I cannot guarantee a perfect performance, but I do pledge to be honest about my failures. Why would I try to hide them anyway, since He knows them all, long before I can even see them myself?

I understand that such a lack of a guarantee would be a deal breaker for most people, but I do not think that is the case with our good Lord. After all, does He not indeed expect, and require, us to move forward through our lives, and our battles, with confidence in Him, and no traditional guarantee at all, except His Word, and His Trustworthiness? If He were to try to explain it all to us in detail, we could not comprehend it. I guess the only reasonable thing to do is to trust His good intent toward us, and step boldly forward, no matter if our hands want to shake a little bit when we first start out. We know He can, indeed, do ALL things, so we only need to know that He cares enough about each of us, individually, to cover our individual needs. Now, the problem for me is to be able to more accurately discern, as the good Lord defines these terms, the distinction between my needs, versus my wants. The hidden aspect of that problem, and the real challenge, is to humbly accept His correct definition, instead of my own distorted version. Help me, Lord!

SPEEDY TRIAL

The man was trembling, with nervous sweat pouring out of him all over, and his face was pale, and his lips quivering. His mouth was too dry to be able to speak, and he could not have managed more than a puny little squeak, even so. Even as slippery as the sweat had made his skin, the steel grip of each of his two captors never failed, or weakened. They marched him, struggling uselessly, straight up to the foot of the Throne. Even though the two angels were about fourteen feet tall, they were still like little miniatures, compared to the One that sat upon the Throne. His mighty toes were visible, glowing like white-hot iron, just like all the rest of His skin. Even His toes seemed to be about three hundred feet tall. The rest of Him faded into the vast distance overhead, lost in a blinding blaze of light around His Head.

A Great Voice thundered, "Let the Prosecutor read the charges!"

A mighty man, one of the children of Light, flew down swiftly, using enormous, strong wings, and landed smoothly about twenty feet in front of the captive, facing him. Even though the man did not wear a nametag, the prisoner knew instantly that the Prosecutor was Moses, though he had never seen his face before.

"Because of envy of your brother, the prophet Abel, and your selfish pride and anger when God accepted his sacrifice instead of yours, you agreed with the devil that Abel should be killed, and you brutally murdered him in his sleep, killing him with the same walking staff that Abel had made and given to you. You are the first human to commit murder, and a disgrace to all humanity!"

When Moses had first begun to speak, Cain's eyes flared with anger and resentment, but by the time Moses had finished his second statement, Cain's head was hung, his eyes upon the ground, since he knew they were right about all of it. He knew what was coming next, too, and his legs began to tremble and give way, but the angels held him upright, and still.

Moses watched him a moment, thoughtfully, and then asked, "Does the accused wish to make a statement?"

Cain looked up at Moses, started to speak, stopped, and, after he quietly cleared his throat, he spoke, just louder than a whisper, "I was wrong. I am very, very sorry." Then he dropped his head again, in shame.

After a few seconds, Moses said, "Because you did not obey the truth, but worshipped your own pride, and gave into envy, and rage, you are guilty of sin, worthy of death. Since you ignored the Word of God, in both the Holy Scripture, and also the Son of God, Who is the Word Made Flesh, you do not have His

Body, or His Blood, to clean your sin. You are guilty of shedding innocent blood, and disregarding Holy Blood. Your sentence comes from the One Who Sits upon the Throne!"

Immediately, the Great Voice thundered again, and said, "DEATH!"

As the two angels instantly flew up into the air, to carry Cain and throw him into the Lake of Fire, he began to cry and beg for mercy, but no one listened.

Moses said, with a soft note of sadness in his voice, "He that gives no mercy shall receive no mercy." As hard-edged as Moses could be, it still broke his heart to think of any human being going to suffer until final death, after full punishment for their sins had been done, through agony and death. Nonetheless, God had truly meant business, when He said to do unto others, as you would have done unto yourself.

ONE WAY OUT

It was the hardest thing any of them would ever have to do. It was one thing to meet an enemy in battle, with one simple objective, to kill before being killed. It was a whole different concept, when the people one had to dispatch were his own family.

The alternative was unthinkable. There was not a single one of them that could tolerate the thought of his own wife, or any of his children, spending years and years of torture and abuse, at the heartless hands of the Romans. It was better to pray for the good Lord to understand, and forgive, than to trust vainly in the mercies of the animal Romans, that had spent centuries inventing horrible ways to torture and kill people. No, at this point in time, the only escape hatch available was the grave. Everyone knew that the Romans would be able to smash through into the fortress the next day. Many of the people were too afraid to just end it by jumping off of the thousand-foot high mountain.

The good Lord had specifically told the Hebrews how to humanely kill the animals that were used in the ritual sacrifices, which brought a swift and virtually painless death, by smoothly severing the jugular, which caused immediate unconsciousness, and the dying was able to pass peacefully, without torment. Every man there, upon Masada, and most of their wives, too, agreed that it was much better to end it overnight, mercifully, and quietly, denying the beastly Romans the cruel savagery they would otherwise commit. Many of the children were frightened anyway, and did not fully understand the issues involved, nor could they possibly imagine what the adults all knew. Not a single adult wanted to hand over their precious children to be violently abused for years by the hell-Romans.

So, a little after supper, the leaders of the Hebrews went to the farthest end of the mesa, and decided just how they were going to accomplish a terrible, but wonderful thing. They prayed. They wept. They encouraged each other, and finally, after an hour, they chose the fifty strongest and most battle-experienced warriors among them, and the one priest that was there, and he quietly and quickly reminded them of the proper techniques to be used in the grim mission. No one wanted the women and children to suffer any longer, after years of fear and despair.

The priest was also a very serious Christian, and had been kicked out of the synagogue, after confessing Jesus Christ as the Son of God. He still took his calling to heart, but now he had been explaining the fulfillment of Scripture, in the life and Person of Jesus Christ. A sincere Christian will only kill to protect an innocent life, or to execute justice and stop evil. Before sunrise, both goals would be achieved, but the executioners would bear the hardest load. They would have to watch themselves and the rest of the fifty soldiers kill women and children, young and old alike, including everyone there, excluding themselves, until the very end. The warriors steeled themselves, knowing the need, and began the grim work, as the people gathered together in their families, waiting their turn until one of the warriors could work through the crowd to them. They kept the torches out, except at a far distance. Darkness was a mercy for those waiting their turn. The people all sang psalms, and prayed, trusting in the Lord, and the gentle warriors that were quietly helping them escape the madness of the Romans.

By midnight, everyone else was dispatched, except only the warriors, and the priest. The men were quietly crying, and some, even of the toughest of them, were vomiting out the supper that they had eaten a few hours earlier, when everyone else was still alive. Each soldier had killed his own family, a responsibility, and honor, which they had to do.

After a little while, the priest led them in prayer, all of them upon their knees in the torchlight, with their bloodstained arms reaching up to God in the night. They wept as they prayed for forgiveness, and gave thanks that at least no Roman hands would defile their loved ones.

One of the warriors was also a very sincere Christian, and he and the priest had already agreed before sundown, that they would be the last two. As the priest continued to lead the men in psalms, and prayer, the soldier quietly rose to his feet, and swiftly and smoothly, went around the large circle, from right to left, gently releasing his fellow soldiers into the deep, peaceful rest that all of them needed tonight. Each man knew what was happening, and not a single one of them struggled, or moved away from the blade of mercy.

Another hour passed this way, and then only the soldier and the priest were left, facing each other in the torchlight. The two men smiled, a quiet, sad smile, and prayed together once more.

The priest said, "I love you, Brother."

The soldier replied, "I love you, too, Brother."

The two men stepped close to each other, and each one hugged his brother with his left hand, and, at precisely the same moment, each one swiftly drew his blade along the side of his friend's throat. They both lost consciousness instantly, and fell right there, side by side, to finish dying peacefully, together. The torch continued alone for some time, and then it, too, flickered, and went out.

SECOND CHANCE

At first, the man thought it was his fevered mind, dreaming up sights and sounds in his delirium. After three nights and two days in the absolute darkness, up to his waist in slime and reeking parts of decaying, half-digested fish fragments, one might think he had grown used to the choking, thick, cold air, so foul that every breath made him want to vomit. The only reason breathing was still even possible was because the chamber where he was jailed had enough air trapped inside it that he had been just barely able to endure through these endless hours, seeming like eternal darkness. He was weak from hunger, but would not eat the pieces of fish that he felt all around him in the water. Fortunately for him, only he was still alive in that water. Also, fortunately for him, when the great fish had swallowed him whole, along with that water, they had been near the outflow of a large river, which dumped enough fresh water into the mix, so that it was far less salty than normal sea water. Normal sea water would have dehydrated him further, and driven his mind completely, chemically, insane. Thirst was a matter of high priority, however, and he had finally had to force himself to choke down a mouthful of the poisonous soup before he died of thirst. It had taken him almost two whole days to take a drink. This man had a stubborn streak that was legendary.

It had been his stubborn streak that had gotten him here. He only dimly recalled his former life, hundreds of miles away, in the court of the nation of Israel. He was an official advisor to the king, and was often a guest at the king's dinner table. The king had even given him a small house near the palace, and servants to attend to his needs.

That all changed in the middle of one moonlit night in the early spring, when a stranger had suddenly appeared in his dream, a Man glowing with white light, from head to toe, and a Face that shined brighter than the Sun at noonday! The Man looked him in the eye, or rather, in the soul, and he began to tremble in terror, still deep asleep, but he could not wake up, and somehow he knew it would not change anything about the vision, even if he did wake up. This was real, more real than solid rock, and the Man was real. He could have reached out a hand, and touched Him, if he had not been shaking violently with fear.

The Man said, in a Voice like a roaring waterfall, that he was commanded to arise at once, pack his bag, and depart immediately, without word to anyone. He was commanded to go straight to Nineveh, and preach the Scriptures, and order the wicked Ninevites to cease their idolatries, and worship the True God, the

God of Israel. The people of Nineveh were famous for human sacrifices, and the more hellish and terrible, the better they liked doing it. They were followers of an ancient religion called Zoroastrianism, and cannibalism of their enemies was a part of the deal. Similar to another pervert people, the Minoans, they often ate their captives alive, and slowly, in public ceremonies. Hebrew captives were their victims of choice, since for the last hundred years, under the reigns of David, and Solomon, and Rehoboam, the people of Israel had become the bitter envy of all the other nations within hundreds of miles.

Jonah recoiled at the command, and protested, claiming that, even if given an army to escort him there and back again, the people of Nineveh were too mighty and too cruel to survive. The glowing Man said, nonetheless Jonah was still going to go, and alone, too, with not even a travel companion. "I will go with you!" the Man said firmly.

Jonah asked Him, "Who are You?"

The Man smiled, and answered, "Until I become born into the world, I am called Melchisedek. After that, I will be called Emmanuel, and Yeshua Messiah!"

As soon as he had said this, the Man vanished, leaving a persistent afterimage in the eyes of Jonah, confirming that the Man had really been there, since a vision does not leave an afterglow, but a real source of light does.

Jonah had indeed jumped up in terror, in a cold sweat, his heart racing, his pulse pounding in his temples, and the Man's Words echoing in his mind. Nineveh?

Jonah had grabbed his bag, after dressing rapidly, and grabbing a few gold coins he had stashed for emergencies, and headed quietly out of the gate of the city. The guards all knew him as the advisor and prophet to the king, and they instantly opened the gate to him, without a single word, and only a nod of respect and recognition, as the old prophet passed quietly out into the darkness. They would not have dared to stop the king, and they were even more afraid of a real prophet. Jonah had a reputation for a hot temper, and some had died when they tried to oppose him. Jonah had not laid a finger upon them. He had said, "Drop dead!" and they had. No one dared to stand in his way, day or night, not even Rehoboam.

As he walked out, away from Jerusalem, terror began to grow again in his heart. Nineveh? Anywhere but that! His skin crawled as he remembered the stories they had heard. Maybe he just needed a little time to think it over. After all, the people of Nineveh had been already evil for many years, so what was all the rush?

He rationalized the whole thing in his mind, trying to convince himself that the Lord would understand, if he took a short little vacation cruise first, to rest from all the activities at court, and gather his strength before tackling Nineveh. Before too long he found himself buying passage on a boat. That plan went sour very soon, once Jonah realized that his disobedience unto the Lord had not only jeopardized his own life, but the lives of all these young sailors on board with him, many of whom he had learned were new fathers, with small children waiting for them back at home. He immediately admitted that the cause of their danger was him, and told them to throw him overboard. He would have just jumped, but knew he might hesitate, and might try to reason his way out of it all again. No, it had to be done, so they had to help him jump.

They finally agreed, and did, and the huge fish appeared under him in the water, and swallowed him whole, along with a lot of small fish, and an enormous bubble of air. Darkness and terror gripped him, and he thought, "Why? I confessed my sin, now why kill me anyway?"

Three days later he heard that Voice again, and opened his salt encrusted eyes a bit, and saw the same glowing Man inside the fish with him. "You know I ought to just let you die here, don't you?"

Jonah would have smiled, if his salt cracked lips could have done so. "You consider NOT killing me?"

"Of course, I do. I would not have come here, otherwise."

Suddenly the fish broke the surface, in very shallow water, and with a monstrous heave of it's stomach muscles, forcibly ejected Jonah and all the stinking fish pieces, and almost all of the water, right up onto a little rock ledge on the shore. Jonah sat up, blinking in the sudden light of late afternoon, and scraped the slime off of him, as he watched the great fish, with a split second of deep eye contact, turn and disappear into the sea.

As he slowly stood up, and looked for a path up to higher ground, he heard the Voice again in his thoughts. "Remember, I will be with you."

Jonah took a long, shaky breath, then let it out, releasing all of the fear and tension that had become so normal in these last many hours. He looked up to Heaven, and this time answered "Yes, Lord! Whatever You want! Which way is Nineveh?"

EINSTEIN DID NOT BELIEVE IN BLACK HOLES

Even though his own mathematics proved the existence of the invisible monsters of gravity, Albert Einstein was offended at the notion, and thought that "nature" should not allow such a thing to exist. What he forgot to factor into his math was the truth, which is that "nature" only does what Almighty God tells it, or allows it, to do, and nothing else. Einstein also forgot that, with God, nothing shall be impossible.

The brilliant Albert was deceived by the same stumbling block that puts blinders on the sight of almost every one of us. We think we actually can understand things which we can observe and measure, which fools us all into thinking that we can theorize and understand the things which we cannot directly observe, or measure. This echoes a strange connection to the Heisenberg uncertainty principle, which claims that it is impossible to precisely measure both the position and the velocity of any particle, simultaneously. We can measure the speed, but the not the position. Or, we can measure the position, but then not the speed. Such imprecision in the thing intellectuals call "science" causes one to wonder, at both of the definitions, as applied, to "science" and "intellectual". Just how smart are we, really, and just how much of that is our vain grasping at straws, so we do not feel so helpless, and ignorant?

Over the centuries, this has led to alchemy, flat Earth, leeches, drowning to detect witchcraft, the Spanish Inquisition, Galileo's mistreatment, horoscopes, the Tarot, surgeons with unwashed hands, the "un-split-able" atom, entire nations and cultures mass-murdering entire other nations and cultures, and a whole endless river of needless suffering and death, for millions, if not billions, of our fellow humans.

It has also, most unfortunately, led to the nonsense started by Darwin, as though a lump of mud, even with an electrical spark, could somehow magically shape itself into the amazingly complex, and elaborately structured, single living cell. Paley shot that down, with his watchmaker argument. Nothing ever changes for the better, unless God causes the change.

In the realm of "hard science" like physics, and cosmology, it has led to such ridiculous notions as "dark matter" and "dark energy" that were only dreamed up by so-called scientists to cover their terrible lack of understanding. They have even spun the yarn about an infinite number of "alternate universes" to cover up their lack of comprehension. They ignored the truth that all things are built out of light, and they cannot even tell you for certain if light should be considered as a wave, or considered as a particle, or why it only travels at a set speed limit. They forgot one of the cardinal rules that Einstein, at least, always kept in mind.

The measurement still has to be corrected for the effect experienced by the field within which the measuring instrument operates. It's harder to accurately guess the speed of a moving train, if the one doing the guessing is riding on the train itself. Even more so, if the observer is in a speedboat, going upstream, or downstream, in a rapidly moving river, the problem with precision escalates intensely.

Because we are imbedded within the gravity well of the monster black hole at the center of the Milky Way, our measurements cannot be trusted. The intense curvature and warping of space and time, which are produced by the gravitational field of the beast, far exceed what we estimate, with our puny little

Earth-based instruments. To accurately measure the total warp and so forth would require that the observer be far enough removed out of the gravity well of the Milky Way, so as to no longer be intensely affected by the gravity. This would reduce the accuracy of the measuring devices, because of distance from the subject.

Why do the scientists fabricate all of these imaginary things like dark matter, and dark energy, and extra dimensions, and superstrings, and all such, and spend billions trying to find one simple bacteria on Mars? They are afraid to look like fools, or admit that they do not have all the answers, or that men will never, in this world, fully understand the things that only God can understand.

At the present time in human history, the only Human Who knows the precise and accurate truth of the nature of Reality is Jesus. If you wish to understand more, study, and ask Him to help you to understand the correct truth of things, and trust Him to do it. You still have to do your own part, though, and study, and learn. Remember: science can tell you, or at least scientists can calculate, or estimate, or at least guess, how many, how much, how far, how heavy, how hot, how cold, how long, how short, and so forth. All of that stuff is indeed fascinating.

If you want to seek a deeper understanding, however, you must seek the Lord. He's the only One that can help you to understand the greatest knowledge, anyway, which is, to know "why?"

BIRTHDAY

They had asked him about it one time. Since John was the youngest, still a teenager, he often times asked the simple questions all of the rest of the men wanted to ask, but were hesitant, to perhaps appear ignorant, just by asking a question. After all, were they, or were they not, the followers of the Son of God? If so, then weren't they supposed to understand the mysteries about Him?

John was young enough and open enough to ask questions about almost anything, and, even if he did not, Peter was certainly bold enough to speak his mind to anyone, anywhere, anytime, even when not too appropriate on some occasions. So that when it happened, it was simple, and natural. It was after they had been with Him for most of a year.

One afternoon, John said, "By the way, Master, just when is Your Birthday?"

Jesus had immediately smiled a warm, quiet smile back at John, glanced around at all of them a second, and said, mysteriously, "On the tenth day, of the first month, of year one." As they puzzled over that for a few seconds, He had sighed, a long, deep, sad sigh, and then smiled again, and said, "Also, on the tenth day, of the first month, of year thirty-three." Then He fell silent, as He watched the beautiful sunset with them.

A couple of years later, it was early on the morning of His thirty-third birthday, but no one on Earth was planning any sort of party for Him. People in this world do not plan parties for dead men, other than funerals. A few of His closest family, and friends, and followers, were planning to honor His remains with spices and fragrant oils, but those were the honors given to departed loved ones, not living men. Nonetheless, there were tremendous plans already long ago completed to celebrate THIS particular birthday of THIS particular Man. It was the very first birthday of its' kind that had ever happened, in all of time and eternity. It was like nothing else ever known before, or since.

It was still dark outside the tomb. He was asleep, in a slumber so deep that nothing in this world could awaken Him. He had been absolutely exhausted, after the ordeal unto death upon the cross, and after that, the brief yet energetic split-second combat with the devil, and then the three days and nights of preaching and teaching the souls trapped in hell, working miracles among them while dragging the broken devil around like a stuffed animal, making it sit there and listen quietly all the time. The three days of preaching had been the most tiring part of the whole week, but then He had a lot of lost souls to reach there, and only three days to convince them.

The first thing He noticed down within the deep, still quietness of death was His

Father's Voice, in His mind and heart. "Son, wake up! Happy Birthday!"

As Jesus heard the last Words, He jumped up off of the stone slab, passing right through the shroud and the head band, which still remained tied together in a knot, but just dropped down flat onto the slab, just like the shroud had done, after He had passed through them. The split second He had awakened, the power of the surge of eternal life returning into His body had stretched out the shroud flat above and below His body, parallel, and suspended in mid-air, as His body was also, at first. The cloth appeared for a few seconds like two floating pieces of plywood, one above, and one below, His floating body.

As He leaped up and landed, solidly and perfectly balanced, He saw two mighty cherubs, glowing brightly in the tomb, one each standing at the head and at the foot of the stone slab. Gabriel was standing where His head had been, and

Michael was standing where the feet had been. That location was perfectly appropriate, since Gabriel was the cherub of time, and always went before the face of Jesus, to announce the time of His arrival. Also, Michael was the cherub of space, and the military high commander of all of the military might of Heaven, and it was his job to ensure that wherever Jesus set His feet was friendly territory, and that the devil was kept out of the area, especially during special operations.

Jesus was glad to be up and moving again, and His friends the cherubs were thrilled to see Him awake again, too, even though they had just escorted Him, as His honor guard, all the way to hell, and three days later escorted Him all the way back up to the tomb, for a short nap, before He had to wake up His body again. As brilliant as the dazzling glow from the two cherubs was, inside the tomb, His Own glow was orders of magnitude greater. If His Resurrection had occurred outside, especially since it was still before dawn, the flash of light would have terrified everyone within thousands of miles, since, for a brief moment, it was much brighter than the sun. That intensity of life and light reactivating His flesh was the same light that burned His negative photo-imprint into the cloth of the Shroud of Turin, which left behind for all of us miraculous evidence of just what happened behind closed tomb doors, early one spring morning. It is still not possible for modern science to duplicate the burned-in image, so there is no possible way that it could be anything but real. The same morning that the Son of God celebrated His first birthday from the dead, He also left all of us a majestic gift in the Shroud, and left behind a proof and visual evidence of the most spectacular miracle since time began!

ANCIENT DREAMS, NEWBORN VISIONS

The good Lord said that it will come to pass in the last days, that He will pour out of His Spirit on all flesh, and that our old men will dream dreams; our young men will see visions. This phrase used to confuse me some, until one day, when wondering about it, my understanding was opened a bit, and I realized the hidden humor inherent in that prophecy. Suddenly, I could see that the old men sleep a lot more than the young ones, and so the message often arrives to the old men as a dream. The good Lord sends the message whenever He thinks that it is the right time. If the target of the transmission is awake, the message arrives in the form of a vision, or if asleep, then, as a dream.

Just very recently, in the last couple of weeks, the understanding has been expanded a little more, to reveal a whole new perspective. Another dimensional viewpoint is perhaps to also remember that when anyone is in Christ, the same is a NEW creature, and the old has passed away. If our old man died upon the Cross with our King, then we are now alive with Him by having been freely given re-birth to everlasting life.

Jesus also explained that the Lord Holy Spirit, when He arrived, would convict the world of sin, of righteousness, and of judgment. Of sin, because they do not believe in Jesus: of righteousness, because He went to the Father: and of judgment, because the devil is judged. Jesus also explained that the Father had committed ALL judgment into the hands of the Son, Jesus, because He is also the son of man. When the Holy Spirit convicts a man, or woman, or child, of sin, He often times does it by a guilty conscience, and some times He does it with troubling dreams. These messages, sent to an unbeliever, are loving warnings, meant to save the person's soul, by inducing confession, and true repentance (or change) unto obedience.

When a person, only by the generous grace of God, is allowed to humble themselves before God, and confess their sin unto Him, and ask forgiveness, and also forgive others that brought hurt to them, and begin to live a whole new life, obeying the commands of Jesus, then the Holy Spirit opens entire new visions, and never seen before wide horizons, to the new believer, and obedient follower, of Jesus. So, the new or "young" man sees visions, much brighter than the dark dreams, from which he has been released, those terrible torments that were a part of his life in sin, as the old man of the world that he once was.

It is reasonable to consider that the most ancient dream ever dreamed was the original dream of Creation, that Almighty God dreamed initially, which culminated in the full completion of the Garden of Eden, with Adam, and Eve, and all the animals. That was God's dream come true, and that of mankind, also.

History records that the devil warped that dream come true into a nightmare, and a twisted lie, instead of the truth.

History also records that the morning of the third day, after the devil thought, mistakenly, that it had won a final victory over God, the strange and magnificent miracle happened, when a newly re-born from the dead, newly raised from the tomb, King of Kings, the Lord Jesus, walked out into the world again, leaving behind the grave. In doing that, He proved for all eternity His supreme power over death, and the grave, and broke the neck of sin forever! Until Jesus returns, to openly claim His rightful Throne over the Earth, there will not be shown forth a greater fulfillment of the newborn vision of God's dream, once more restored upon the Earth, and lasting peace between mankind and God. God has always been at peace with us, or we would already be dead.

THE STONES CRY OUT

Modern science has proven over the last two centuries that the human body is constructed of precisely the same materials that can be found abundantly in the Earth. Our bodies are truly made of the dust of the Earth.

Some of those chemicals and their atomic components had to be formed in the ultra-furnaces that are created when stars become supernovae. Those internal pressures and insanely high levels of heat that are generated in the center of exploding stars form altogether new atoms, that are bigger, heavier, and much more complex that the original hydrogen and helium, which comprised almost all of the stars' original mass. As the explosion scatters the new atoms far and wide, they are swept up and gathered into newly forming stars, and solar systems, and planets, like Earth, but not one other planet in the entire universe exists, where men can walk around, and stay alive, not for more than a few seconds, or perhaps minutes, if equipped with a space suit.

Since the only significant difference between a boulder of granite, and a wind-blown, microscopic, dust-spec of granite, is a matter of scale, and mass, it can be correctly defined that all solid matter upon the Earth is, except for difference in scale and mass, some sort of stone. That does even include the nano-sized dust particles way up in the stratosphere, too. Even though our bodies are flexible and soft, they are still basically built of many small, very, very small, stones.

Whenever we living human beings, in our bodies made of many, many exceedingly small stones, give thanks, and honor, and glory to Jesus, the Holy Begotten Son of Almighty God, then we are fulfilling the prophecy which Jesus gave us as He rode upon the little gray donkey, His mighty war-steed, that

Monday of Destiny, when He entered Jerusalem to re-claim it for God.

The children had been praising Him and welcoming Him to His Own capital city, and His Own Kingdom, as He rode in that Day, mistakenly called Palm Sunday for centuries. The Pharisees told Him that the little ones should keep silent, but Jesus responded that if these did keep silent, then the very stones would cry out to worship Him!

We are the stones which cry out! Hosanna! Baruk Habab Hashim Adoni!!!

THE GADARENE EVANGELIST

The disciples were stunned into silence. Even though they had just seen the Lord Jesus, their friend and leader, command the raging storm winds, and the wildly crashing waves to sit down, and shut up, and then suddenly had also seen the wind and the water immediately sit down, and shut up, this was too much for them. Even though right after that, they had watched Him directly order a couple of thousand demons to instantly exit a man which the demons were holding hostage, and then instantly seen, with their own eyes, as the evil angels left the man, through the top of his head, like a dark, polluted stream of sewage, and then flew directly into a nearby herd of swine, this last thing was still a jaw-dropper.

After all, Jesus was very well known here, since it was His Own childhood hometown. On the way there, He had healed a woman of a long term illness and internal bleeding, and also raised, back to life, a little 12 year old girl that had died. He had fed five thousand men, plus women and children, starting with only five barley loaves, and two fish, and everyone was full when done, and they had more left over than when they started.

None of that seemed to count much in the eyes of the nasty old "nay-sayers" from His old village. They said, in essence, "Who does this Guy think that He is?" They thought that just because they had watched Him grow up, right there in front of them, that He could not possibly be the real Messiah. None the less, Jesus did whatever He could do to heal the sick ones there, but was limited by the rules, of the principles of His Ministry, which required Him to work

His greatest miracles in direct response to the proportion of faith which the believer invested in Jesus. Therefore, only little faith permitted only little miracles.

It was also at about this time that Herod the maniac murdered John the Baptist. With the hostile reception His old childhood neighbors had shown to Him, and then, with the sudden horrible murder of John, second cousin to Jesus, it was time for an immediate break. Jesus sent His disciples ahead in the boat, to cross over to the other side of the Sea, but He Himself withdrew to a nearby mountain, overlooking the Sea, perhaps Mount Carmel. As He prayed, and spoke with the Father, and listened to the Father, He looked out over the moonlit Sea of Galilee, and saw His disciples in the boat, straining at their oars, since the wind in their faces was so strong.

Jesus knew that it would be daylight again in another hour, so He immediately moved, with a single miraculous step, from the mountainside, to the surface of the Sea, just astern, and a little off to the starboard side, of the disciples' boat. He figured He would just go ahead and walk on ahead of them to the shore, and stretch His tired legs along the way, and meet them there. It would have worked out just that way, too, if not for the fact, that at just the right moment, the wind blew the clouds clear of the moon, and some of the crew on the boat saw Him out there walking calmly on top of the water, as though upon dry, solid ground, His feet not even slipping any with His solid steps, like one would expect from water. The water did not splash away from His feet, either, but just stayed solid right where He touched it, like instant granite.

As soon as they saw Him, they shouted out, terrified, thinking they had seen a ghost. He altered course, and began to walk calmly over the water toward them. Peter, whose faith was bold, at least, as long as he was focused upon Jesus, jumped out of the boat, obeying Jesus when He was commanded to join Him upon the waves. As soon as Peter was distracted by the howling wind, and the heaving waves around them, he began again to doubt, and started to sink, but Jesus reached out and grabbed Peter, saving him from drowning. They both then climbed into the boat, and Jesus immediately transported the boat, by a miracle, to the shore, where they all climbed happily out onto land.

The land where they beached was the country of the Gadarenes, where just a couple of weeks earlier, Jesus had driven thousands of demons out of a man that had been infested with them, and He had told the man to go tell people what great things the Lord had done for him. That same man was standing upon the beach, greeting them the moment they landed, and with him were several other local people. They welcomed the sailors, and gave them warm, dry blankets, food, and goats' milk, and water to drink. These people had been very frightened of Jesus during His last visit, but the Gadarene preacher had told them all, in exquisite detail, how wonderful it felt to be a human being once again, and not just a helpless dungeon captive, constantly tortured from the inside out by the hell-animal demons that would not leave, until Jesus kicked them out. It was not just his preaching words that convinced them. Everyone around knew about the man, and it was truly a miracle every day to see and hear the entirely restored man living out his new life in a very thoroughly sane and positive manner. When he had been infested with the filth, the evil spirits had broken chains used to try to bind him, so he would do no harm to anyone, but once Jesus kicked them all out forever, all of the invisible chains of captivity and oppression were removed from the man and his entire life. The man became a new creature in Christ.

For the next several days after his healing was given, the preacher stayed, and obeyed Jesus, telling everyone who would listen just how magnificent Jesus really was, and that they should try to meet Him as soon as they could. The man, in his restored and fervent state, was extraordinarily convincing, and very many people began to believe that maybe that Stranger, that had so helped this fellow, should be studied a bit closer.

The result was, that not only those upon the beach that early morning with the Gadarene preacher, but also almost the entire region of the Gadarenes, became converted, and came seeking Jesus, to know Him, and be saved by Him, and be healed by Him, and learn from Him, and trust, and love, and follow, and obey Him.

As for the demons, they had been granted some limited escape permission by Jesus, to go into the herd of pigs, and had instantly done it. Even though the pig is considered unclean to eat, still, it is a living creature, and not inherently evil in itself. The Lord knew what would happen, and that was why He allowed the demons into the pigs, because the sudden invasion into the pigs' minds of horrid, twisted, insane evil, in the persons of the demons, instantly drove the pigs mad with fear and terror, and, to escape it, they ran instinctively headfirst into the Sea, and drowned. As they died in the water, the demons were forced out, and had no other permission, from Jesus, to remain in the world, anywhere, and so were instantly forced out into the "Outer Darkness". This is a region of reality outside of Creation, where exists only eternal, absolute darkness, and absolute cold, much colder than what we understand as absolute zero. It is a zone of Nothing-at-All, except for cold and dark, so extremely cold and dark, that human minds cannot comprehend it.

Even an evil angel, or demon, is a living creature, made to live in light, by a God Who is Living Light. The agony of being entombed alive, in absolute cold and darkness, and having no way to die, to escape the misery, is a tough thing even for an evil angel to endure. No wonder they had begged Him not to send them there. If they had not spent years tormenting His new preacher, and then, after that, slaughtered 2,000 innocent animals, by terrifying them into madness, and suicide, maybe He would have let them go somewhere else. When the demons had first seen Him, they had come and acknowledged that He was the Son of God. Somewhere in the encounter, the evil angels forgot that Jesus will not long tolerate the abuse of His followers, but will fully repay it. They also forgot that no one can trick Him, or manipulate Him into doing anything at all.

A FEW OF THE STRANGEST DREAMS

It always seemed to me as though the very oddest, of all the mysterious dreams, with which our good Lord has graced me in my years, had to be those which eventually somehow came true. The symbolism and metaphoric images in the dreams looked so congruent with the real world things my eyes and ears ultimately saw, and heard, that the probabilities are mathematically impossible for these several parallels to be random coincidence.

I will sincerely try, to the very most accurate recollection, to describe as precisely as I am able the ones which stick in memory. I will describe the dream, then how it seemed to be made real at some future point in time. They will not be listed strictly chronologically, since I will write them in the order in which the good Lord recalls them to me now, as I write this story.

The first chapter in this book is about the first dream that I can remember. There indeed came a time in my life in which I was literally surrounded by snakes, in a pond, a little after midnight, with a full moon. My crazy friend Rick and I had decided that a little midnight dip was just the thing on a hot July night at Rick and Sharon's farm one Texas summer evening. We swung out over the water on a rope swing, then dropped in with a huge splash, and made very sure that we splashed around a whole lot when we started toward the bank of the pond. We figured the more noise we made, the further away from us the water moccasins would swim. I never thought until sometime later about the rattlers along the banks, which would have been worse, if one of them had gotten us. There was also another time or two in my life where I was truly surrounded by deadly enemies, and would have been destroyed, if not for the Lord.

There was the time one of my 8-month old kittens came running up to stand beside me in a dream, and when I looked down, I saw that someone or some thing had placed a rubber band on the kitten, like a gag on a person, around the back of his little head, and stuck deep across the mouth, making it very uncomfortable, and impossible for him to close his mouth all the way, and he could not take it off of himself. I immediately tried to reach down and pull it off of him, but for some reason, I could not reach him. I told a friend of mine that I had a dream, where someone was trying to hurt my kittens, and I could not stop it. My friend said a thing which later confirmed that he was sadly lacking in any sort of spiritual perception, and woefully short of deeper understanding. We are no longer friends, because the Lord commands us to go from the presence of a man, when we do not perceive in him the lips of knowledge.

Anyway, what he said was that it was that it was only a dream, unless I let it become anything more than that. How foolish! Within another month, raccoons from the nearby creek had killed one of my kittens, the precise same one that came running up to me in the dream, and two weeks after that, they killed another one of his brothers, too. Since the solid-as-a-rock raccoons just laughed at my BB gun, and they were too damn smart for me to catch them in my humane trap, even though the skunks and opossums were caught, many of them, I had to do something, or lose the remaining three cats. So, I bought a 22, set a ¾ inch plywood board against the garage, as a bullet-proof safety backstop, shined a very bright light on it, placed a plastic plate, with cat food, in front of the plywood there, and waited in the shadows. I got tired of staying up all night waiting for them, so I rigged a motion sensor to turn on a radio in my bedroom whenever anything came in through the little gap in the back gate, and then woke up for battle whenever I heard the rock and roll start up. Eventually, although some success was obtained, the final effective solution was when the good Lord gave me my ¾ wolf, Lobo. One morning a year ago, I found a dead raccoon in the back yard. Lobo was standing there by it, wagging his tail in victory and pride, for a job well done!

There was the dream, in which my home, which is located on a corner, had seemed to become some type of corner gas station, and there were crooked people trying to sneak in and steal anything that was not bolted down. I had to watch the front, the sides, and the back corners continually, and was always on guard to stop criminals. Not long after that dream, I built an 8-foot tall security fence around my yard and home. Within a few years after that, our neighborhood was hit with a rash of break-ins and thefts, which even got so bad that people were being held up when they went out to walk their dogs, and a few citizens even were hurt. Things have settled down again, for now, but I am still very glad that I wisely heeded the warning of the dream, and built my fence when I did.

There was the dream, where I was in some sort of a room along a hallway, and the hallway was well-lit, but the room was dark, and I saw myself standing at the door of the room, looking out into the hallway, and, sometimes, speaking with people as they passed by the door, but, somehow, I was not able to go beyond the threshold of the room, out into the hallway. The exception was that upon two unique occasions, I was somehow carried, or rolled, like on a cart, out into the hallway, and into an elevator, and down many floors, for some mysterious purpose, and then carried, or rolled, on one of the occasions, back into the room again. It all seemed to last forever, and I wanted to leave the room, and go places, and do things, but I could not.

Approximately four years after I remember having that dream, my appendix burst, and I did not realize I was in serious trouble, and did not go to the hospital for another ten days. I was near death from internal poison, and was given emergency surgery, in which they cut me open from just below my heart, all the way down, way past my belt. They took out some damaged things, and patched up the rest as best they could, and by the grace of the good Lord, I still live, nine years later. I was in the hospital almost six weeks, healing from being sliced apart, then being stapled back together, and having poison and infection killed off, and drained out of me. The room in the dream was the hospital room, and the two trips down the elevator were when they took me down the first time, to do the surgery, and when they took me down the second time, almost six weeks later, to let my next door neighbor bring me home.

The dream described in "Carnival of Cruelty" also has come true, as the Lord, over the years, released me from alcohol, tobacco, and other bad habits as well.

The dream described in "Shock" also came true, since the girlfriend mentioned there almost completely destroyed my life, on her way out of it. I forgive her, but I do not want to see her again, until Heaven!

The dream described in "The Cabin" also has come true, at least so far, since I did, in truth, come inside, close the door, and write. I also did not give up. At least, I have not given up, yet. I hope that I do not. I hope I can find the backpack by the door when the moment comes that I need it. I hope I get to take my dog, Lobo, with me, wherever we go.

In my first book, there is story named "Crown of Light" that describes the dreams I have had of the Great White Throne Judgment. I believe that one will come true, but not until the Lord has completed fulfilling every single one of His unbreakable prophecies. Remember, He is also the King of Prophets, too.

It is a scary thing for me to experience, every time something occurs, and I remember a dream in which events very parallel to real-world things was given to me beforehand. The Lord said He told the things that would happen before they happened, so that when those things which He prophesied did actually occur, we would know for certain, that it was Him, the Living truth, which did it. Since I am convinced that He is the Living Truth, He does not need to prove it to me. I think He does it for me sometimes to warn me, and sometimes just to confirm to me that these strange dreams and ideas which are being crafted into stories and

books really are from Him, and not just
my own fevered imagination.

There are very many more such
dreams which have happened to me, that
later on, did come true, with enough
commonality of similar events, people,
surroundings, timings, and outcomes, that
it is impossible for me to not be
absolutely certain that the dreams are
indeed sent by Some One, Who cares a
lot about me, and takes good care of me,
even if I do tend to get on His nerves at
times. He always forgives me. At least,
He always has, so far!

The very favorite, future dream/vision
that I have ever had is the one described
in "Family Reunion". That is the most
realistic of all the dreams I ever had. It is
the most-hoped-for future moment, of
which I am aware. What a Day, when we
join with our Lord Jesus, at the seventh
trump, after the tribulation is almost
completely over! Any remaining
Christians, which did not die during the

tribulation, will join with all other believers, still alive, or just then resurrected, as we rise into to the air, to meet with our God and King! It is because I know what He shows me is true, and also because it is so wonderful, and exciting, that it makes it difficult to wait, and to work on here, in what will someday be considered the ancient past, someday way down the road, far into the future, when time has ended, and eternity reappeared, openly.

TODAY, ALL I CAN SEE ARE BEAMS

Sometimes, there are days when it seems to me that everyone (and I do mean everyone, including me) is doing things all wrong. The rude woman at the cash register, and the crazy dude, in the old wreck of a pickup, that almost took out a bunch of us, at around 65 miles per hour (us, not him) and the absurdly argumentative client, that does not want to yield even a shred of respect, or cooperative spirit, are just a few examples that pop readily into my mind. I am very sure that you likely have some folks like them in your own memory, even though it might be more pleasant to forget them. There are days in which it feels like I am experiencing an endless parade, of jerks, and selfish fools.

It would be very discouraging (for those trying sincerely to honor the Lord, and His goodness to us, by doing what good we are able) except that the good Lord, in His infinite wisdom, and mercy, sends a little refreshing breeze, and a clean breath of fresh air, just when you have about given up hope of ever finding any kind, intelligent people walking around out there. Just about that time, as you are taking your couple of small bags of groceries to your car, you see a sweet little old lady, being very, very careful to move her empty shopping cart out from between our two cars, watching every single little move herself, slowly guiding her cart out. When our eyes met, we both smiled, and I thanked her for her excellent courtesy, and her fine behavior. She smiled even bigger, and said that she would not want someone to scratch her car, so she did not want to scratch someone else's, either.

Also, for every bad, dangerous driver, who makes a stupid move, and causes trouble for others, if you watch for it, you can also notice several very good, intelligent, responsible, and polite drivers, who make up for the jerks. For every rude client you must handle, you can perhaps notice something wonderful that one of your co-workers did, to help out someone else. It helps to disengage from the front row seat of the emotional agitation, and a quick way to help do that, is to sort of keep score, of, maybe, bad drivers, versus good drivers, while you are driving to, or from, work. When you turn it into a game, it becomes an interesting spectator sport, instead of your being down there on the field, helmet to helmet, waiting for the next snap. Instead of planning to out move them in traffic, just keep driving correctly, and mentally check the scoreboard in your head. Which is winning, foolishness, or wisdom?

Another principle at work, which is a bit more uncomfortable to remind ourselves, is that we are told clearly that whatever fault we perceive in someone else, is most likely one of our own particular failings, also. If we see a man acting lustfully, do we ever stop to think that we also have had some secret thoughts about someone else? Perhaps we would not be so quick to fire a shot at someone else's behavior, if we can just take a deep breath, and remember that we also are not very perfect people. Even if our personal failings, or rebellions, are different than those of the people that we think poorly about, we still would not be escaping the fire, either, if the good Lord, in His infinite mercy, had not allowed us to believe in Him, so His sacrifice could cover our own personal sins! Are we not a fine bunch of little hypocrites?

Our excellent King, Jesus, instructed us to very humble, and deeply honest, especially with ourselves, when it came to pointing out another person's flaw. He told us to speak the truth, in love, and to seek reconciliation, through genuine change, and obedience. He told us to be, first, accurate, to remove the beam from our own eye, and then we can see clearly to remove the speck from our brother's eye. I have come to realize that whenever I see fault in someone else, the correct response is not, "Lord, change that person!" The more accurate prayer would be, "Lord, please help me to get these beams out of my eyes, so we can help someone else to get the speck out of theirs!"

THE MISSILE SHILOH (HIGH PRECISION KINETICS)

In every military conflict since primitive times, the most effective weaponry, if applied strategically, is usually the deciding factor in the final outcome of the clash. One famous historical example is the ending of World War II by the strategic application of newly-invented nuclear weapons. Extreme, yes, and also extremely effective, is a verdict already self-proven.

Oh, of course it is romantic fantasy, and absolute nonsense, for people to attempt to accept as fact those tales where the hero is somehow able to overcome even things like overwhelming numbers of opponents, though that did occur in historical fact more than once, with Samson. It is usually absurd to expect the hero to somehow survive unhurt, and maybe even un-hit, while right in the middle of a hailstorm of live bullets, but that happened at least twice to George Washington, once early in his gun wielding days, and also, later in his active battle career.

Most often, it is either overwhelming odds, or superior weaponry, or a combination of those, which is the decider. Some historical exceptions which pop into mind are Afghanistan, back in the old days against the Russians, or under the Taliban, or now, apparently, and ever more increasingly, against the Americans.

No matter how effective a weapon is, it will do no good without a delivery system, and the more precise, the better. This same principle applies to almost all weapon systems, from a thrown rock, to a locked-on-target missile. This has caused the invention and development of all sorts of high powered sights on guns, and heat-seeking missiles, and computer targeted and guided nuclear warheads. This concept of weapon design and application even can be seen in computer viruses, made to do all sorts of evil mischief, but useless without effective delivery to target. Make the weapon get there, and do not miss, and then destroy the target.

The most effective weapon would be one that could see the target clearly, identify it correctly, get to ground zero without being stopped, and detonate destructively enough to annihilate the target, even at the cost of the weapon itself. If it could also be achieved in a manner which does not cause friendly fire type casualties, that is doing it the highest class way possible. The only thing possibly more excellent than that is if the target knew what its' destiny was, and voluntarily chose to go on and do it anyway, since the required strategic total victory could not be attained any other way. That way, there would only be one friendly loss, and the greater in effective magnitude, therefore, would be the victory won.

It's simple math, but it comes with an outlandish price tag, if the one friendly loss is the King of our side. That, if nothing else, itself, would be hellishly wrong, if He had not voluntarily chosen to do it to spare all of us, instead of His Own Life. I am very glad that the Father of Lights gave Him back to us again.

The simple strategic aspect was that sin was what had to be destroyed, not just the devil that started it. It would be a simple act, indeed, for Almighty God to immediately vaporize the devil, but that would not kill evil, or the effects, or continued practice of evil. Once the contamination set in and spread, there was only one solution. Sin had to be sterilized out of the world, like a dangerous killer plague, which it really is.

The only absolutely effective and unstoppable killer of sin had to be Someone, Who was absolutely righteous. The penalty for sin is death. Someone had to die because of your sin. Yes, it was because of my sin, too. Because our dying to pay for our own sins would only have fulfilled justice, it did not fully reveal God, as also showing mercy. So, in order to achieve a new, forgiven life for me, and yes, for you, too, God had to become a Man, and live without any sin, and die innocent, Himself, so He could cover the penalty for my sin. Yes, it was for your sin, too.

He also had to do it willingly, since for starters, no one, at all, can ever force God to do anything, at all. Besides that, God considers it an abomination for anyone to sacrifice a human life, if the death is forced unwilling against the victim. The thing Jesus did for us was voluntary, the greatest possible act of unselfish love any Man could ever do. It is only rivaled for excellence by the sacrifice that the Father made to send Jesus to die for us, and the sacrifice that the Lord Holy Spirit makes on a continual abiding with those of us who are, indeed, saved, but still are very imperfect in our walk with Him. It must not be very much fun for the Holy Spirit to have to watch me and listen to me whenever some person (that I would love to call an idiot) pulls out in front of me, nearly causing a wreck.

Jesus was the unstoppable weapon, and the unbeatable delivery system, all rolled into One. He did not miss His designated target, and did indeed, single-handedly, shatter evil forever. He got right to ground zero, and detonated, and it cost Him His Own Life, and pain I cannot imagine. It also gave me a new life that I never could have imagined, either.

Jesus Christ was, and is forever, the Missile Shiloh!

FULL COLOR MEMORIES FROM A LITTLE GRAY LIFE

The children were playing a game with a ball, and were thoroughly enjoying themselves. There were about two dozen of them, and they were absorbing the excellent, bright spring day. No one was trying to cheat, but everyone, boys and girls alike, was doing his or her best to actually win the game. There was some good natured shoving and jostling, but nobody tried to hurt anyone else. The incidental contacts were more friendly gestures than moves designed to hurt, or incapacitate. This was recess, the way recess was always meant to be. The teachers had sent them outside for an hour to work up an appetite before lunch, and to burn off some of the restlessness that a morning of intense studies had produced in them. After all, they were still children.

They had been hard at the sports, running and chasing the ball all over the large open schoolyard, for about 20 minutes, when a very large, strong, and beautiful pure white horse came trotting quietly up toward them. One of the boys saw him, and shouted "Tzedek-Sus!" The other children also saw him, and ran toward him, all shouting his unusual name (se-DEK-soos) as they ran, laughing, to meet him. This mighty horse was very well known here, and for that matter, everywhere that existed. This war stallion was the personal mount for King Jesus the Christ, the unconquerable King of Kings. Neither the horse, nor the Man, ever lost a fight, either in that ancient dim time, thousands of years in the past, or now in this world-to-come, where nobody was left alive that was evil. There were no more enemies for the King of Kings, or His warhorse, to have to fight and kill, since all of them had already died and turned into smoke and ashes in the lake of fire. All but the devil, that is, that still had many more centuries of pain and suffering left that he had to repay back to God, for all the insanity that he had caused in the ancient time. Eventually, he would finally pay it all off, every tiny bit of it, and then God would finally let the devil die, too, so no one evil would ultimately be left. God never intended to torture any person, or any thing, for all eternity. He is not sadistic, or unjust. Still, He will have His books balanced completely, at the final end. God is living Justice, and that is why He named His Own horse "Justice-Horse". That's the interpretation of Tzedek-Sus.

"Tell us a story, tell us a story, about the ancient time, Tzedek-Sus!" All the children loved the great horse, and they loved to listen to him tell them about things that happened long ago, in the times of war, and death, and pain. These children, born entirely into a new, sinless world, where the King of Heaven walked among men, and the entire new Earth was like the Garden of Eden, again, had never been sick, or sad, or afraid, or lonely, or suffered any of the horrible things that had happened to children before the devil was locked down in the lake of fire. They knew of things from history, since they had to study them in school, so that no one could ever be stupid enough to try sin again. Even so, it was only a vague, abstract thing for them to consider any hurtful thing, since none of them had ever experienced any such thing in this world.

The mighty, winged super-horse tossed his giant head and extremely long, thick mane, neck muscles rippling as he did. He whinnied out a loud, horse-type laugh, and said, "All right, just one. It can't be a long one, though, since you all have to go eat lunch in a little while."

As the children gathered around him, and sat down eagerly on the grass to listen, the horse said, "I will tell you the true story, about someone I knew back in the ancient time, and what happened to him. I will tell the story about the Day that the donkey danced!"

When he paused for a deep breath, the children let out a bunch of "oooos" and "aaahs" in anticipation.

"In the ancient time, as you know from school, people often times did crazy things, bad things, things that hurt themselves, and sometimes even other people, too. This was because of the thing called sin, which made every one see things crookedly, and so act wrongly. If you put on a blindfold, and try to walk across a canyon, on a tightrope, you will not fare very well. You must be able to see clearly where to correctly place each foot step, so you do not fall. It is not like this today, but in those times, if you fell a long way, you would get hurt, or even maybe die."

"Then one day, the good Lord sent His only begotten Son to help the good people, so the bad ones would not win by cheating, which is what sin really amounts to. The Son of God did not come into the world to destroy men's lives, but to find, and save, the lost. All of you know the One that I am talking about. He is my Master, and yours, too. King Jesus!" Every child nodded, and smiled at the mention of His Name.

"Well, the first thing He had to do was make sure that He told them precisely why He had come, and also, because men's hearts were hardened by sin, and their minds were confused by pride, He found it necessary to actually prove it to them, about just Who He really was, and what was going on. He did this by working many, many miracles, more than all other prophets had ever done, all put together. He also did this by what He said, since Hs Word has the power to save, and to heal."

"This initial stage of preparation for His attack against evil took a while, about three long years, to be accurate. This phase was more correctly considered the rescue part of the mission, so that people would understand when He achieved His final victory over death and sin."

"There at last arrived a Day, foretold since the beginning, when the King knew it was time for the frontal assault He had been planning all along. He did not send His entire army, the whole Army of Heaven. He only sent Himself into the battle. He did not send in His army, because He knew He was able to beat evil all alone, without anyone, or anything, helping Him."

"The enemy's headquarters was at Jerusalem in those days. The devil had so corrupted God's chosen people that even their priests thought that they were holy, but actually they were worshipping, and serving, the devil. King Jesus would not tolerate the enemy to continue to occupy His Own capital city."

"The very worst of His enemies at that time were not the Romans, even though they were the ones that unfairly murdered Him. It was not even the crazy, evil high priests of the Jews, though they were the ones that framed Him unjustly, and arranged His death, and actually screamed out loud again, and again, for His death, all because they were envious of Him. His worst enemies were the devil, and all the other evil spirits, the crooked angels, and anything in the unseen zone of Creation, if that thing was trying to hurt or kill His little brothers and sisters. Jesus always took His family responsibilities very, very seriously. He would never abandon a brother or sister to death, not if He could do anything to stop it, even if it cost Him His Own Life, instead, which it did."

"So, upon this wonderful Day of Days, a day foretold for many centuries, the King sent two of His followers a couple of miles away to a nearby village that perched on one side of the Mount of Olives, a town named Bethspage. When they arrived, they went straight to a house they had been told to find, and began to untie a young adult boy donkey. It was early in the morning, just at sunrise, and the people who owned the colt came out to see what was happening. When the men said the colt was required by the King of Kings, the owners gave permission, and the little gray donkey was taken to meet the King, Who was Jesus."

"When Jesus and the donkey first saw each other, it was like old friends that had been apart, and missed each other much. There was a couple of minutes of close one-on-one contact, and direct mind-to-mind communication, and the young donkey suddenly, enthusiastically, nodded his gray head, and brayed "Donk-EY! Donk-EY! Donk-EY!"

"A little while later, after a huge breakfast for everybody, Jesus and the disciples all walked toward Jerusalem, about two miles away from the house of Lazarus, in Bethany, where they had all gathered for the giant breakfast. They knew they had a big Day ahead. As they walked they talked of things to come, and Jesus led the donkey, with a light hand upon his gray back. When the two had met that morning, Jesus had placed His hand upon the donkey's back, right at the shoulders, in the center of the back, and, when he had lifted up His hand, a minute or so later, the donkey's back showed a charcoal colored cross running down and across his back, right at the shoulders. Donkeys to this very day still all have the dark cross on their backs, made into the fur. The little gray donkey was marked to carry the Word of God."

"When they reached the edge of the city of Jerusalem, Jesus took off His sandals, and climbed onto the back of the little gray donkey, where the disciples had placed their cloaks to make a padded saddle for Him. He was also wearing the robe of a high priest, woven from the top, throughout, without seam."

"The people along the sides of the street, and there were almost two million of them, since they had arrived from all over the world, for Passover, began to chant and sing praises to God in the highest! They also took not only some of their own cloaks, and other shawls, and such, and tossed them before the feet of the donkey, they also laid down palm leaves all along the road for Him to ride upon, so even His donkey's feet would not get dirty!"

"When the donkey heard all of the people singing "Hosanna!" and "Baruk Hashim Adoni!" his little heart was racing a thousand miles an hour! He wanted to stay calm, and carry the King with regal dignity, but he just couldn't help it, and for a few seconds, his feet pranced nimbly and swiftly along, as if he was about to explode right up into the air!"

"The donkey calmed down instantly, but still had a happy donkey smile on his little gray face. His nerves settled perfectly, when he heard Jesus laugh, a happy, good natured laugh, and heard Him say, "I understand. It's okay. We're almost to the Temple. Just a couple of more minutes, all right?"

Just at that moment, one of the teachers came out and said, "Children, come to lunch!" Some of the children got up right away, but more wanted the great horse to keep on with his story.

"Now, young folks, we must not keep the cooks waiting, since they were so kind as to make a great lunch for you all. We can continue the story next time. I promise that it has yet more excitement to come, and a couple of rough spots, but a very happy ending indeed!"

As all of the children got up obediently to begin to walk back to the lunch hall, one little boy stopped a moment, and said, "Tzedek-Sus, how come you know so much about the little gray donkey, and how things felt for him that day?"

The horse smiled, and nodded, then snorted, and said, after pawing the ground in mirth a few times, "I told you it was about someone I once knew. I know how he felt, because I was that little gray donkey!"

Tzedek-Sus said, "Look!" As he said this, he turned around, and spread his enormous wings, and then reared up on his powerful back legs, showing his entire back at once to the little boy. The boy gasped in wonder and smiled with delight. There, right in the middle of his huge white back, right between the great wings, was a golden cross made into the fur of the horse!

ABOUT THE AUTHOR, AND LOBO

Lobo was given to me about three years ago, about the time I began to write these stories. During this long journey from the first story, all the way to now, with the completion of book number three, there have been many times when I wanted to quit, and to just quit fighting for it. No matter what else was going on, Lobo was always with me, as close as he could snuggle, and guarded both me, and our cat, Cheetah, and even killed a raccoon that came into the yard one night, so it could not hurt little Cheetah.

Lobo has been one of the very finest gifts our good Lord ever shared with me. There is no way I can ever repay his goodness and loyalty, though I do try. The Lord will always be number one in my heart, but Lobo runs Him a close second. That wonderful creature, three-fourths wolf, and one-fourth shepherd, has behaved like a fur-covered guardian angel with me. I think our good Lord gave Lobo to me so I could see, and feel, and hear, and smell, and touch, and know His love for me in a solid, real manner.

GOD'S LITTLE NANO-BOTS

Have you ever had the mental picture of Almighty God as some sort of giant, mysterious scientist, working late at night, in a small laboratory called Earth, with an experimental test subject He calls humans? In the 21st century men can, and do make microscopic sized machines, called "nano-bots", that are many times smaller than the thickness of a human hair. They are programmed to do all sorts of things on a tiny scale, where ordinary medicines, surgeries, and other types of remedies or repairs are not possible. The little machines are marvelous, but are not aware of the scientists.

God calls us His children, and tells us that He loves us. He sent His Son to save us, and the Holy Spirit to keep us. He sends us, many of us, dreams and visions. He walks with us, and helps us walk with

Him. He promises us promotion beyond comprehension someday. We are not robots, but children. We love You too, Father!

www.ingramcontent.com/pod-product-compliance
Lightning Source LLC
Chambersburg PA
CBHW050359030726
47503CB00006B/1926